'Why don't [...]
you really ar [...]

Shaken, Terise [...]
anger—for which [...]
blame him—seemed to accentuate his maleness.

She could hardly believe the thoughts tumbling through her mind. How could she be thinking of him as anything but an enemy at this moment? She knew only that enmity was the last thing she felt.

He angled himself across the corner of his desk and picked up a red folder marked 'Confidential'. She waited tensely while he flicked through the contents...

Valerie Parv was a successful journalist and non-fiction writer until she began writing for Mills & Boon in 1982. Born in Shropshire, England, she grew up in Australia and now lives with her cartoonist husband and their cat—the office manager—in Sydney, New South Wales. She is a keen futurist, a *Star Trek* enthusiast, and her interests include travelling, restoring dolls' houses and entertaining friends. Writing romance novels affirms her belief in love and happy endings.

Recent titles by the same author:

PS I LOVE YOU
A RELUCTANT ATTRACTION

SISTER OF THE BRIDE

BY
VALERIE PARV

MILLS & BOON

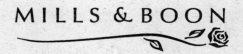

*All the characters in this book have no existence outside the imagination
of the author, and have no relation whatsoever to anyone bearing the
same name or names. They are not even distantly inspired by any
individual known or unknown to the author, and all the incidents are
pure invention.*

*MILLS & BOON and the Rose Device
are trademarks of the publisher.
Harlequin Mills & Boon Limited,
Eton House, 18-24 Paradise Road, Richmond, Surrey TW9 1SR*

© Valerie Parv 1996

ISBN 0 263 79428 8

*Set in Times Roman 11 on 12 pt.
01-9603-46138 C1*

Made and printed in Great Britain

CHAPTER ONE

CHAOS reigned in the ground floor conference room of the Westmore Building. As fast as workers aligned rows of chairs they were disarranged by hordes of media people, scrambling for the best positions for themselves, their microphones and cameras.

The press conference was due to start in a few minutes. As yet there was no sign of Ryan Westmore himself, but the supercharged atmosphere suggested that he would take his place on the cable-strewn podium very soon.

Intending to tuck herself inconspicuously into a back row to observe proceedings, Terise O'Neill was startled to have a foot-high stack of folders thrust into her arms. 'Thank goodness you're here.'

Around the stack she glimpsed a petite figure, clad in a dress-for-success cream linen suit. The girl had harried young features under a shock of close-cropped red hair. Terise stammered, 'I'm sorry, I don't——'

Fingers brushed hers in greeting. 'Forgive me for rushing you when you've just arrived, Miss Ferris, but I'm swamped. I'm Debbie, the executive receptionist. Sue didn't mean to drop you in the middle of a war zone like this, but neither did she plan to go into premature labour. I'm doing the best I can, but I'm no executive secretary.'

Neither was Terise, although Debbie had obviously mistaken her for one. Still clutching the folders, she wavered. Should she point out Debbie's mistake, and risk being asked to leave without seeing Ryan Westmore, or play along until her curiosity was satisfied? Seeing him was vitally important.

Curiosity won. 'What shall I do with these?'

Sighing her relief, Debbie gestured towards the throng. 'Hand out these press kits then field questions until Mr Westmore arrives.' She glanced at her watch. 'He's due in four and a half minutes and he's *always* on time.'

Which rather fitted Terise's preconception of him as a work-driven tyrant. Handing out the folders gave her the appearance of belonging there, which was an unexpected bonus, although she recoiled from the consequences of inevitable discovery. She hated scenes, and this one would be a lulu when Ryan Westmore found out that his Miss Ferris was really Terise Diane O'Neill. If it hadn't been for Clair...

It still hurt to think that she was dead. Two years younger than Terise, she had been a vivacious blonde whirlwind, soaking up life's experiences as a sponge did water. She possessed—had possessed—the exact opposite of Terise's sober, get-the-facts-first approach to living.

Now she was gone, and Terise wanted to know why. The only person who could tell her was Ryan Westmore.

Her anger flared anew, white-hot, cauterising her fear of crashing Ryan Westmore's press conference. She had come to see what sort of a monster he was, and fate had handed her the perfect means. What happened afterwards would be well worth it.

'How highly does Westmore rate Sydney's chances of hosting the next international trade assembly?' one of the journalists asked, relieving her of a folder.

Safe ground at least. Last night's newspaper story about Australia's chances of securing the prestige trade event was what had alerted Terise to the conference. At the invitation of the Australian government, Ryan Westmore was masterminding the Sydney bid.

'He rates them very highly, but cautions against over-confidence,' she quoted from the article, hoping that the journalist wasn't getting his own words back at him. 'Any more questions you have will be answered shortly.'

'How're you coping?' Debbie materialised at her elbow as she gave out the last press kit.

'Surviving.' Non-committal seemed safest. 'What else needs doing?' Please, Lord, not computers— or anything else she wasn't qualified to tackle, she prayed silently.

'You could do a microphone check. Sue usually does it to settle things down so Mr Westmore can get right to the point.'

Thanking whatever angels looked after kindergarten teachers, she headed for the microphones. Years of MC-ing Christmas concerts and parent-teacher nights had inured her to such technical matters.

But not to dying of stage fright, unfortunately. Butterflies still did aerobics in her stomach at the thought of appearing in public, but they were hidden under a veneer of confidence. It was thin enough to scratch with a fingernail, but—thank goodness—no one had tried yet.

As Debbie had anticipated, Terise's appearance at the microphones resulted in quiet attentiveness. She gulped, recognising several television reporters, but got through the test by pretending to be the real Miss Ferris—no doubt a high-powered executive-type, who ate gatherings like this for breakfast.

Her peripheral vision was suddenly filled by a man waiting with barely leashed impatience at the door nearest the podium.

Ryan Westmore.

If she hadn't seen him, Terise suspected she would have *felt* his presence nearby. He radiated power the way the sun did a corona.

His pictures didn't do him justice, she thought. They only hinted at a powerhouse physique which seemed almost physically threatening in the flesh. Or was it the piratical way he stood in the wings, long legs slightly apart, like a sea captain athwart his bridge? His photos made him look hard and uncompromising. In person his strong features and the distractingly sensual curve to his mouth suggested that he could do a great deal of compromising if he chose to.

The slight tap of his notes against a muscular leg brought her to her senses. Her Miss Ferris persona managed to lean towards the bank of microphones and say, 'Ladies and gentlemen, Mr Ryan Westmore.'

His taut nod acknowledged the polite applause as he strode to the podium. His glance grazed her in passing, and she drew a sharp breath at what she saw. His eyes burned with an intelligence and purpose which awed her. *This* was the man she wanted to hurt as he'd hurt her stepsister? Taking on a great white pointer shark would make more sense.

As if he sensed her inner turmoil, Ryan Westmore spared her a second more thoughtful appraisal. She could almost hear him wondering what she was doing here, reaching a conclusion and dismissing her, all in the space of a heartbeat.

The dismissal stung, but managed to strengthen her sense of purpose. He might be formidable but he wasn't invincible. It shouldn't be impossible to find some scandal she could link with his name, damaging his chances of the knighthood expected to be his when the bid succeeded. Poetic justice indeed.

Her knees shook, and a swallow did nothing to ease her dry throat as she reached the sanctuary of a side alcove. Watching the man in action might reveal some weakness she could use against him.

Weakness? She almost laughed aloud at the idea as the press conference proceeded. Ryan Westmore treated the assembled media as an orchestra, with himself as conductor. What should have been a media feeding-frenzy turned into an hour-long commercial for the trade assembly bid.

The toughest questions were answered with consummate skill and disarming frankness. When Terise caught herself hanging on to every word, a savage anger ripped through her. His charisma disguised an evil man—couldn't they see that?

'He's amazing, isn't he?' With a sigh bordering on hero-worship, Debbie joined Terise in the alcove, dashing her hopes of slipping away unnoticed before the conference ended.

'Very impressive.'

The shakiness in her voice earned a sympathetic smile. 'I know he can be intimidating but don't worry. Sue recommended you highly. She meant to ease you into the routine herself, but——' she consulted her watch ' —about now she's kind of busy. She should have listened to the doctor when she said first babies sometimes come early.'

The pieces started to fall into place. Obviously Sue was Ryan Westmore's personal assistant and Miss Ferris was to replace her during maternity leave.

Terise had barely had time to speculate about Ryan's relationship with the new baby when Debbie added, 'Luckily I had time to tack your name on to the card when I sent flowers to Sue and her husband. Knowing you're here will set her mind at rest.'

So the child wasn't the product of an affair with his secretary. Pity. It would have fitted his image as a heartless Lothario. Clair had suggested as much in her letter, but Terise might have known that an office romance was too obvious.

'Everything's under control here. Why don't I show you around while we have a minute?' Debbie proposed.

There was no alternative but to follow Debbie to the executive lift, which whisked them to the highest office level—one floor below the penthouse suite which, she informed Terise, was Mr Westmore's Sydney residence.

'Where does he normally live?'

She shrugged. 'He has several homes, but his favourite is Westmoreland—a property at Bowral in the southern highlands.'

Her comment stirred a painful memory. Clair's last letter to Terise had come from there. She and Ryan had spent much of their married life at the property, although Clair had hated it. 'It's like being buried alive,' she'd written, adding, 'If possible, it's more conservative than Port Macquarie.'

This was the home town they'd shared after Clair's mother had married Terise's father. Clair's widowed mother, a teacher, had moved to the country out of economic necessity. Odd to think that it had been Terise's undisciplined behaviour in class which had brought them together. Even odder that she had settled down and become a teacher herself.

Clair had been the opposite—a good student who had then caught up with Terise in spades when she'd reached her teens, surpassing her stepsister's worst escapades.

When she'd run away to the city it had seemed like a relief to the family. They hadn't known she'd even met Ryan Westmore—far less married him— until four years afterwards, when desperation over Ryan's cruelty had moved her to write to Terise.

She'd been pregnant when they married, and too ashamed to write sooner, she'd explained. Terise couldn't imagine Clair being ashamed of her actions. It suggested a measure of the desperation Ryan Westmore must have driven her to.

It had taken Terise some months to reorganise her life and come to Sydney, only to find that Clair had been involved in a fatal car accident. The cavalry had arrived too late. Forgiving herself was a long way off still.

'This is your office, and that door leads to the boss's inner sanctum,' Debbie was saying.

Terise had left the lift, and followed the woman around the office on autopilot.

'If you need anything, ask me. The conference ends in fifteen minutes and Mr Westmore will brief you on anything urgent when he returns. Until then, Sue left some notes for you on the computer.'

A shaky smile was all Terise could muster. 'Very efficient, our Sue.'

Debbie smiled. 'I forgot that you two know each other. Is that how you got hired so quickly?'

'You can be lucky sometimes.'

She grinned. 'I wonder if you'll still think so at seven o'clock tonight.'

'I thought the workday ended at five?'

'Maybe for human beings with lives outside the company,' said Debbie. Then, looking faintly alarmed at her own temerity, she withdrew and closed the door.

The message was obvious. Human beings with lives outside the company didn't include Ryan Westmore. The man was not only a monster but a slave-driver as well. Charming.

Since the real Miss Ferris could arrive at any moment, Terise decided that she'd better make the most of the twist of fate which had given her access to Ryan Westmore's private office.

All the same, she hesitated before opening his door, half expecting him to be waiting behind the vast marble slab which comprised his desk. Like everything else in the room it was black. An appropriate colour for a black-hearted man.

The matt black bulk of a compact filing system loomed in his office, seductively accessible. Heading for it, she came up short, aware of eyes boring into her. It was only a portrait, and humiliation washed over her in waves at her foolishness.

If she hadn't just seen the subject for herself she would have questioned the artist's interpretation. Ryan Westmore was thirty-two, which made this a recent portrait. It exactly captured his fiercely aquiline features, which would have been scholarly on a less prepossessing man, as well as the intensity in the steel-grey eyes—right down to the smoky rim around the irises. Terise felt as if the painting was looking at her, not the other way around.

The eyes seemed to follow her to the files. The trade assembly material was far more voluminous than she'd expected. Even a cursory inspection would take time.

'Good. You're reviewing the files I requested.'

The brisk statement, delivered in a vibrant baritone voice, chilled her into immobility. Debbie had said he was punctual but he was five minutes early, damn him.

'Welcome to the company, Miss Ferris,' he said, crossing the office with purposeful strides and sliding behind the desk. He must have been an athlete at some time, to move so economically.

The Zegna suit was expertly tailored, and hinted at muscles sculpted by hard and conscientious use. The hints were enough to leave her mouth arid. He'd been quoted as saying good health was a business asset, especially in a chief executive. If so, his body must have been worth a fortune to Westmore Incorporated.

What was it about him which made her mind shoot off at tangents? she thought furiously. Who cared what shape he was in, or how potent his personal charm? It was probably those very qualities which had beguiled Clair into marrying him and making the biggest mistake of her life.

'My name is Terise,' she supplied, since he seemed to expect something from her. Her throat felt so constricted that it was an effort to speak, but he was absorbed in paperwork and didn't seem to notice.

The breath caught in her throat. Why had she given her real first name? Evidently the absent Miss Ferris didn't possess a first name, because he showed no reaction. At least Terise could answer to her own name for now, hopefully for long enough to escape before being unmasked.

Even without Clair's disturbing letters, she didn't fancy being on the receiving end of this man's wrath.. It would be more fun sitting through a cyclone.

'Very well, Terise.' A faint smile lifted the corners of his full mouth. Finding that she was staring, she looked away. Such a smile should be declared a lethal weapon. Knowing what kind of man he was hadn't prepared her for the impact of his personality. No wonder Clair had found it impossible to fight him.

The fog lifted long enough for Terise to register his look of wry amusement. He gestured to the files fanned in her hands. 'Wouldn't you be more comfortable reading those in your office?'

Was it going to be this easy? Her face tightened with the effort to remain impassive. 'Of course, Mr Westmore. I don't want to disturb you.'

His eyes travelled lazily over her figure, which was carefully disguised beneath the most businesslike suit she possessed, chosen to blend in at the press conference. Evidently it was not well disguised enough, judging by the frank interest she saw in his eyes.

She knew she wasn't beautiful. An under-developed figure topped by gamine features hardly had model potential, and then there was her hair—a positive cascade of shoulder-length curls which always created the impression that she'd rushed to get where she was going.

The only redeeming feature, she thought, was her colouring. Her genes had kindly combined to provide peach skintones, avocado-green eyes and a hair-colour of soft taupe—like a lion's mane, her father had described it. It hardly warranted the level of attention Ryan was paying her.

'You are disturbing me,' he agreed, unaware of how incredibly mutual the feeling was. He passed a hand over his jaw, as if fighting fatigue. 'But, since you are, does your union permit you to make coffee for me?'

An unwelcome surge of compassion was hastily suppressed. So he was tired. She ought to be cheering. 'How do you like it?' she asked briskly.

'Black, strong. You'll find what you need through there.'

Depositing the files in the outer office, she explored through the door he'd indicated, finding a well-equipped kitchenette. He must work late a lot.

While the coffee brewed she set a tray with bone china cup and saucer, linen napkin and shortbread biscuits from a well-stocked cupboard.

The single cup on the tray brought a questioning look. 'Don't you want some yourself?'

'I thought you didn't care to be disturbed.'

The flint-hard eyes flashed fire. 'This is your first day. I don't want you thinking you've come to work for a slave-driver.'

Guilt washed her features with warmth. Her father always said he could read her face like a book. Ryan was plainly doing so now. 'Have I?' she asked, to distract him.

A smile which wasn't quite a smile lit his sharply defined features, making her limbs weaken unexpectedly. If a smile wreaked so much havoc, what would a kiss do?

Now where had that thought come from?

Angrily she thrust it away, but not before her heart-rate had jumped at the very idea.

His eyebrow lifted again. 'What do you think? *Have* you come to work for a slave-driver?'

Since she hadn't come to work for him at all, she could answer truthfully. 'Not a chance.'

He pushed his cup aside and drew a sheaf of papers towards him. 'Sue chose you well. She knows her replacement won't last long without some spirit.' He looked up briefly, but with soul-searching intensity. 'You'll do.'

Will I, now? she thought furiously as she retreated to the secretary's office, quietly closing the door although she longed to slam it so hard that it rattled on its hinges. Literally shaking with anger, she needed a few minutes to calm down before making any sense of the files.

The red 'Confidential' flags on the front blurred as she tried to sort out her feelings. What was she so angry about? Then she knew. It killed her to respond to Ryan Westmore when Clair had amply forewarned her against him. Sharing even a moment of camaraderie with him was like making a pact with the devil himself.

But who expected the devil to be so attractive? Her chin settled on one hand. He would have to be in order to hijack people's souls the way he had hijacked Clair's.

The memory strengthened her resolve, and she opened the first folder, searching for information to use as a weapon against him.

It wasn't as easy as she'd hoped. Every meeting, every transaction to do with the bid for the world trade assembly was catalogued in minute detail. If there were any slush funds, shady cash deals or underhand dealings they weren't even hinted at here.

The last file closed with a disheartening thump. The kind of thing she needed was unlikely to be openly recorded. It would be stored on his private computer, protected by an impenetrable password.

The secretary's computer was probably linked to his, but without the proper skills she hesitated to turn the thing on. Ryan thought she'd already done so, accessing the instruction to study these particular files. She had gathered that from his re-action to finding her in the file-room. Luckily he hadn't glanced at the screen on the way in and found it incriminatingly blank.

A sense of futility gripped her. Coming here had seemed like a good idea, when Clair's death had fired her with the zeal to make Ryan pay. At the very least Terise wanted people to see that there was another side to their corporate knight in shining armour.

Maybe she should have followed her first impulse, to turn Clair's letters over to the Press and let them investigate. Newspapers thrived on scandal. But without proof all she had were Clair's slightly hysterical accusations.

The folders slid from her fingers as despair washed over her. This had been an insane idea from the beginning. She was about to leave while she still could when an intercom buzzed on the desk and Ryan's voice filtered into the room. 'Miss Ferris, come in here, please.'

Now what? She shrugged on her Miss Ferris persona and headed for his office, stopping to collect a stenographer's pad and pen from the desk. It looked good, and occupied her trembling hands, although she couldn't do shorthand to save her life.

Ryan's face was a granite mask. He indicated a straight-backed chair in front of his desk. 'Sit down.'

Terise thought it prudent to comply. The notepad trembled in her grasp like an autumn leaf about to fall. He watched her for a moment in silence, every second of which was agonising as she waited for the axe to fall. The so-kissable mouth was set in an implacable line which sent tremors of apprehension surging through her. How could she have seen any humanity in such a hard visage?

'I assume you know why you're here.' It wasn't exactly a question. His tone was a sufficient harbinger of doom.

She kept her chin lifted, refusing to let him see how intimidated she felt. 'I can guess.'

He rose, palms flattening against the desk as he towered over her. 'You'd be right. Debbie just got a call from Joanne Ferris, who is caught in a traffic accident on the F4 freeway.' His voice dropped to a soft level which was, if anything, more daunting. 'Now, suppose you explain who you really are and what you're playing at?'

As cover stories went it was woefully inadequate, but it was all she had. 'My real name is Terise O'Neill.' Clair's surname had been Everson, and fortunately she hadn't changed it. 'I'm from the country and came to Sydney looking for work. After reading about your press conference in last night's paper, I meant to approach you about a job.'

His expression didn't soften. 'As a secretary?'

She kept quiet, knowing that her real qualifications would give the lie to her story in an instant.

Again he was ahead of her. Before she could react, he moved around the desk and grasped her arms in a vice-like grip. She would probably have bruises there tomorrow.

Her stumbling progress barely kept pace with him as he towed her to the outer office, thrusting her into a chair in front of the computer. She stared at it as he loomed over her, arms crossed. 'Well?'

Her fumbling fingers finally found the on-switch and the screen glimmered into life. So far, so good. 'What shall I type?' she brazened.

' "The quick brown fox" will do fine.'

Her index fingers stabbed at the keyboard, producing a mess of gibberish which fooled neither of them. She let her hands drop.

'So you aren't a secretary. Surprise, surprise.' The velvet tones were mild, but she sensed the anger he held in check by force of will. 'What precisely are you?'

She gulped, and finally offered him the truth. 'In big trouble.'

A storm gathered behind his eyes but she kept hers level with his by pretending to be Miss Ferris again. She wouldn't have been afraid of anyone—not even the devil disguised as Ryan Westmore.

A grudging respect crept over his features, but there was no lenience in his voice. 'I'll say this for you, Terise O'Neill, you have a lot of nerve. Who sent you? One of the other bid committees?'

'Good lord, no.'

'Then who?'

'No one. I told you, I'm looking for a job.'

'And I'm Arnold Schwarzenegger.'

He was big enough and awesome enough. Fragments of Clair's letters spun through her mind. If Terise had had any sense she would have been terrified of him. She would have been if she hadn't been so intent on her mission.

Whatever else he might have said was forestalled when two small, blonde-haired missiles exploded into the office, flinging themselves at Ryan and each taking possession of a Zegna-clad leg. 'Daddy!'

Something totally unexpected tore at Terise's heart. There was no mistaking their identity. They were Clair's children. Their angelic, fair-haired looks were so much an echo of hers that tears burned the backs of her eyes. She blinked them away before Ryan noticed.

The children were followed more sedately by a stout, middle-aged man who looked totally frazzled. 'Sorry about the intrusion, sir. I was taking them upstairs, but they made such a fuss about seeing you first that it seemed safer to accommodate them.'

Ryan's expression had acquired an astonishing forbearance. 'It's all right, Marcus. As a nanny, you're a first-rate chauffeur, and these two minxes are well aware of it.'

The chauffeur must have brought the children from school. He watched in pained impotence as they proceeded to wreak havoc in the small office.

Spying the active computer, one of them reached for the keys, and Ryan made no move to intervene. Reflex and training came to Terise's aid, and her voice automatically dropped into playground-register—what her colleagues called her 'sergeant-major's voice'. 'Stop that at once, missy.'

The child's jaw dropped open and she stared at Terise, but her hand also pulled back from the keyboard. 'My name isn't missy. It's Trudy and I'm six,' she announced, a wary note threading her voice.

'Hello, Trudy, I'm Terise. Bet you're too little to draw a picture for me.'

Her eyes flashed acceptance of the challenge. 'I can so, too. I draw good pictures.'

'Prove it.' Terise handed her some typing paper and a black felt-tipped marker. The child dropped to the carpet and began to draw, pink tongue protruding slightly with concentration.

Not unexpectedly, her twin stopped dipping her hair experimentally into a glass of water and sidled up. 'I'm Lisa. I can draw good, too.'

'Only if you're going to behave. Are you?'

Her butter-wouldn't-melt-in-the-mouth look didn't fool Terise, but she accepted the child's nod. 'Here you are, then. Both of you draw me something you saw on the drive home. I have a chocolate in my bag for each picture.'

Six-year-olds were her speciality, and she'd acted on pure instinct. Energy not properly channelled had to come out somewhere—usually in destructive ways. But distracted they were perfect angels.

Slowly she became aware of Ryan's appraisal. Marcus, the chauffeur, looked at the busy children with open-mouthed amazement. 'Well, I'll be. Where did you get this miracle-worker, Mr Westmore?'

'I'm not a miracle-worker, I'm a teacher. And he hasn't ''got'' me,' she started to add, until she caught a gleam of purpose in Ryan's dark gaze. All too obviously he had something in mind, and his look said that she wasn't going to like it one bit.

'Miss O'Neill is looking for a job,' he said, with a coldness which sent shivers down her spine. 'We'll soon see if she's telling the truth. *Do* you want a job?'

'Of course.' A trap loomed ahead, but she could see no way to avoid it.

'Excellent.' She fancied she heard the sound of metal jaws springing closed. 'Because you've got one. Taking care of these two for me.'

CHAPTER TWO

THE interval between his outrageous proposal and her response was measured in seconds, but it felt like hours. Guiltily she realised that her problem was not only with taking care of Clair's children, it was also with getting involved with their demanding and possibly dangerous father.

His attractiveness had already acted as a warning beacon. Sailor beware! If she hadn't already been warned about him, every instinct she possessed would have done it for her.

Observing him from a safe distance was one thing. Dealing with him at close quarters was quite another. And yet . . . and yet there was that invisible thread of family feeling which had begun winding itself around her heart, connecting her with the two cherubs at her feet, their heads down, small bottoms upraised as they worked on their drawings.

Striving to remain objective, she tore her gaze away from them, unfortunately clashing with the diamond-bright challenge in Ryan's eyes. Warmth surged up her neck, although she willed herself not to blush under his searching scrutiny.

A strange excitement kindled like a brushfire deep inside Terise, answering something in his look. He knew, damn him. Somehow he knew that she would refuse the job and confirm his all too obvious suspicions. It was crazy but she felt reluctant to let him down. Given what she knew about him, it didn't make sense.

'I can't,' she forced herself to say.

'Then your teaching qualifications are spurious too?'

This couldn't be left unchallenged. 'No, they're genuine. I have a diploma in early childhood education from Newcastle College, four years of in-service teaching with infants, and I was a recreationist for a children's hospital.'

'Impressive,' he said, sounding anything but impressed. 'If it's all true.'

The man was infuriating. Having caught her out in one lie he was determined to suspect everything about her. Her blood steamed. 'You can check my references yourself.'

He folded his arms across his broad chest. 'Depend on it.'

His cold assertion jolted her back to reality. Why defend herself so vigorously if she had no intentions of working for him? The jaws of the trap tightened until breathing was an effort. 'It hardly matters unless you employ me,' she stammered, around the huge lump in her throat.

Alerted by the charged atmosphere between the adults, the children were looking up with such luminous cornflower-blue eyes that she felt like a criminal.

'You require a job. I require a nanny. If your qualifications are genuine there should be no problem,' he observed with infuriating logic.

And there wouldn't be if anyone else had offered. But this was Clair's husband, her children.

It would provide the perfect opportunity to establish exactly what had happened, a small voice in Terise's head insisted.

It still felt wrong—even as a purely business arrangement. She tried to tell herself that it would last only until she had her answers, and then she would be free.

Liar, the same small voice mocked. You don't want to be free of him. He intrigues, fascinates, beguiles you in a way no man has done before.

Foolish woman. She was falling into the same trap which had probably caught Clair, the difference being that Terise's eyes were wide open— and still she felt herself falling.

'You're right. I accept the job,' came a whispered acquiescence. It felt as if a stranger had spoken in her place.

He nodded, as if the question had never been in doubt. 'Agreed. Provided your background checks out.'

His persistent scepticism stung in a way she resisted examining too closely. 'It will.'

His steel-grey eyes became hooded, and he steepled long fingers in front of his chest. 'This time I think it will,' he commented drily. 'Where are you staying?'

His question caught her by surprise. 'With my stepmother in Queenscliff.'

Elaine had moved back to the city after Terise's father had died, two years before. She had hoped to be reunited with Clair, but it hadn't happened. For some reason Clair had chosen to contact Terise instead. The burden of her letters weighed heavily. Why hadn't she written to Elaine? How different this scene would have been then.

Ryan's decisive tone invaded her thoughts. 'Marcus will drive you to Queenscliff to collect your things and bring you back here.'

Panic threatened to overwhelm her. Moving into his home, even with the girls as a buffer, was an enormous step. Far too much, too soon. 'I didn't plan to live in,' she said, annoyed at the betraying tremor in her voice. Where was the cool professional now? 'I'd rather stay where I am. I can still work whatever hours you require.'

His bladed hand slashed the air dismissively. 'My working hours are unpredictable. International contacts frequently have to be made in the middle of the night, our time, and I'll be travelling a lot, so this has to be a live-in position.'

Belatedly Terise recalled that she wasn't supposed to know anything about his personal life. 'But surely your wife . . .' The word lodged in her throat, cutting off further speech.

'My wife died in a car accident six months ago,' he stated. Astonishingly there was an edge of pain underlying the bald statement.

Sharing the pain, but unable to let it show, she asked, 'Are there no other relatives to help look after the children?'

'My wife was an orphan, and what relatives I possess are scattered overseas, so we're spectacularly short of family.'

So this was how Clair had explained her family's absence from her wedding and her life. It felt devastating to be denied so totally, however Clair had rationalised it. It didn't lessen Terise's sense of betrayal.

At her feet, the children stirred, once more engrossed in their drawing. Her heart turned over. Not that she needed any reminding, but Ryan had evoked the strongest reason for her to swallow her reluctance and take the job. These children—her family—had lost their mother. They needed Terise.

'I'll be back as soon as I can,' she said shakily, trying not to think too much about what the decision entailed.

At the reception desk, Debbie reddened when she saw Terise, with Marcus close behind her. 'I'm sorry for mixing you up with Miss Ferris. You kind of looked as if you belonged here.'

Ashamed, because it was the impression she'd tried to create, she offered her own apology. 'As it turns out, I *am* working for Mr Westmore—as the children's nanny,' she added.

Debbie's beaming smile made Terise feel worse. 'That's fantastic. It was a lucky mistake after all.'

Depending on how you looked at it. 'Probably,' she agreed. It was kind of Debbie to be so welcoming. At least Terise had one ally in Ryan's camp.

Marcus promised to be another, although he'd probably have befriended anyone who took the children off his hands. His martyrdom at being co-opted into the nanny role was evident as he expertly steered Ryan's silver-grey limousine through the thick traffic towards Queenscliff.

'Never thought I'd be ferrying six-year-olds around,' he grumbled. 'You're here in the nick of time. Another week and I'd have been off.'

'How long have you worked for Mr Westmore?' she asked innocently.

'Eleven years.' He looked shamefaced. 'You got me. I wouldn't have resigned—but I wanted to, plenty of times. Those two are right little handfuls.'

Needing to learn as much about her charges as possible, she queried, 'Is that since their mother died?'

In the driving mirror, his head shook in denial. 'It's been worse since then, but they were difficult beforehand. Mrs Westmore either spoiled them or ignored them. Then, afterwards, Mr Westmore didn't have the heart to be tough on them—not surprisingly. Until you spoke up today, I don't recall anyone saying no to them. Probably gave them the shock of their lives.'

'Not before time.' Recalling how Elaine had spoiled Clair when she was younger, Terise could see how Clair had come by her ideas of motherhood.

'Look at Clair,' Elaine had used to say, catching the teenagers together in some scrape—usually of Clair's devising. 'You can see she's the inno-cent one.'

The suggestion had invariably been that Terise had led her child astray. Just as invariably she'd been punished, by being sent to bed without dinner. Then, perhaps to atone for the injustice, Clair would smuggle food to her during the evening.

A smile curved the corners of Terise's mouth at the memory. It hadn't been Clair's fault that her mother was blind to her flaws—although Terise had often wished that Clair had summoned the courage to confess.

'It wouldn't do any good,' she'd always denied when the possibility had been broached. 'Mum would say I was covering up for you. At least this way I make sure you get something to eat.' Her argument had been so sweetly reasoned that objecting had seemed churlish, even though deep down Terise had still questioned the justice of the situation.

Was she taking this job to make sure the Westmore twins got a fairer deal than she had enjoyed? It seemed likely—until an image of their father sprang into her mind, blurring the scenic beauty of the Manly peninsula as they sped along the Esplanade.

What had she learned about him so far? So much that she didn't want to know—mostly about her own response to him—and so little that she needed to find out. What was it about him that demolished all of her defences, leaving a raw vulnerability she'd never experienced before?

Teachers were trained to show leadership, grace under pressure—all the qualities which deserted her the moment Ryan Westmore's eyes locked with hers.

There was much about him to admire, if only she hadn't known better. Reluctantly she pictured him at the press conference, striding into the room with a poise bordering on arrogance, taking charge of all those journalists and famous TV people, bending them to his will without apparent effort.

Her throat dried at the memory of his touch on her arm, an irresistible force as he'd challenged her to use the computer. She'd been wrong about the bruises. He'd known precisely how much pressure to apply to achieve his aim without physical damage.

Psychological damage was another matter, but he couldn't know how his touch haunted her even now. Wouldn't ever know if she could help it. So he was an attractive, forceful, personable man. They had probably said the same about Jack the Ripper.

Dragging her thoughts back to the present, she directed Marcus to Elaine's apartment building, perched on a clifftop overlooking Queenscliff beach. Luckily her married name appeared on the intercom system at the door, so Marcus had no reason to be suspicious. He might not have connected the name Everson with Clair, but he could have mentioned it to Ryan in passing, and *he* certainly would.

'I'll come up and give you a hand with your belongings,' Marcus volunteered.

Elaine was at a women's club meeting that afternoon, so there was no reason to forestall him. 'Thanks. There isn't a lot. I haven't really unpacked since arriving from the country.'

For this reason the task took little time, and she was soon on her way back to Ryan's building at Circular Quay. She'd left a note telling Elaine about her new live-in job, promising to phone with more details next day when, hopefully, Ryan would be at work and they could talk freely.

Not that Terise intended to tell her much about Ryan. Clair had kept her marriage a secret, and Terise meant to honour that for now. Telling Elaine that Clair was dead would be tough enough when the time came. Distressing her with the truth about Clair's marriage might be avoided altogether.

Clair had written that Ryan was a cruel tyrant of a husband. That he was a tyrant Terise could well believe after today. Although there was no real injury, she fancied that her arm still throbbed where he'd hauled her to the computer to let her humiliate herself. But cruel? It was hard to reconcile that with his actions as a father.

A sigh whispered past her pursed lips. Even bullies loved their mothers, she reminded herself. Serial killers had been known to keep pets. Just because Ryan cared about his children it didn't make him a candidate for sainthood.

'What is Ryan Westmore like to work for?' she asked Marcus as the Harbour Bridge sped by. Maybe he would mention some hint of scandal that she could use as a weapon against Ryan.

The driver's grin cheated her of an answer. 'You'll find out soon enough.'

She sighed. 'I was afraid you'd say that.'

When Marcus deposited her at the penthouse, Ryan was waiting. 'Your qualifications check out,' he said, without preamble.

He hadn't wasted time after she'd left her curriculum vitae with Debbie, at his instigation. 'I told you they would,' she bristled.

His penetrating gaze was momentarily hooded as displeasure furrowed his brow. 'You told me a lot of things which proved to be unreliable.' It was the most diplomatic way anyone had ever called her a liar and she tensed, every nerve on alert, as he added, 'I'm well aware there is more to you than meets the eye.'

Had he found out the truth about her so quickly? She shrugged to dispel the chill working its way down her spine. It had nothing to do with the soft whisper of conditioned air throughout the penthouse. 'What makes you think so?'

'Your background, for one. You supposedly came to Sydney seeking work, yet your previous employer informs me she offered you the position of deputy principal in order to keep you.'

The offer had been stunningly unexpected, but by the time it was made Terise had been committed to leaving. Regret was still a distant companion. 'Maybe I needed a change,' she offered, embarrassed by how inadequate it sounded.

Ryan's disapproval raked her. 'You'd better hope the move to Sydney has satisfied this—restlessness.

My children need stability, not someone who'll up and leave on a whim.'

He had started out by offering her a job that she didn't want. Now that it was being threatened she wanted it very much, though she didn't have the courage to examine her reasons too deeply.

'Four years in my last job hardly makes me a will-o'-the-wisp.' It was hard to keep the sharpness out of her tone, and he looked thunderous as she failed audibly.

Like a caged predator, he prowled to where a wall of glass offered a panoramic view of Sydney Harbour, studying it for long moments before turning back.

The brightness of the harbour waters was reflected in his look, which was blindingly direct. 'Time will tell, won't it?' He came closer. 'What made you choose me in your quest for self-fulfillment?'

Brain whirling, she stood her ground, although every instinct counselled retreat. 'According to your public image, you're a man who gets things done. With so much unemployment in the city, it made more sense to approach someone like you than to answer endless advertisements and join long queues of applicants.'

He was so close that his breath was fragrant on her cheek. A trace of an old scar was woven into the grim line of his jaw, and it was an effort for Terise not to lift a finger to follow its contour.

The devil he might be, but there was something alarmingly compelling about him. The aura he projected was almost hypnotic in its intensity. She felt herself swaying towards him, held still by main force as he continued, 'Out of all the business people in Sydney, you decide I could best help you?'

So was this how a cobra felt, compelled beyond its will to move to the strains of the charmer's flute? What was he getting at? 'I told you, the press conference gave me the idea.'

A strong finger hooked upwards and grazed the side of her face, sending electric impulses all the way to her core. 'And you had no idea I was no longer married?'

He must have discovered the truth. This was all part of some strategy to force a confession from her, she decided. The breath tightened in her chest. 'No, I told you...'

In a move so swift that it blurred before her eyes, he snatched up a newspaper lying on a console nearby, flicking it open at the business page and holding it in front of her.

Heart sinking, she looked. There, alongside the announcement of the press conference, was a picture of Ryan with Clair, who was clearly identified as his 'late wife'.

Two thoughts slammed through Terise's mind virtually together. The first was a prayer of thanks that Elaine wasn't much of a reader and was unlikely to have seen the item. The second was that he *did* know who she was, and that this entire scene was a cat-and-mouse game, with Terise as the mouse.

Wetness misted her eyes—for Clair, for Elaine, for this whole sorry mess about which she could do nothing more. Revenge for Clair would have to rest with fate. Ryan was about to throw her out, making her story about being unemployed humiliatingly authentic.

Though she willed her eyes to dryness, refusing to give him the satisfaction of making her cry, a droplet managed to escape. Astonishingly he caught it with the tip of his finger. 'Tears, Terise? For my situation, or for yourself because I'm on to your game?'

What was the point of prolonging this? 'Go to hell.'

'Stronger souls than you have wished me there,' he said caustically. 'Although it is an odd choice of destination for a honeymoon.'

What was he talking about? 'Honeymoon?'

His nearness heightened her senses, making her dizzily aware of his maleness as he loomed closer. His hand travelled from her cheek to her shoulder, and his fingers dug into the tender flesh.

But it was at his harsh tone that she winced. It was empty of emotion, as if something—or someone—had drained his resources in this area. 'Yes, honeymoon. Why else would you come to me with such a cock-and-bull excuse, if not in hopes of snaring yourself a wealthy husband?'

This time Terise had no need to pretend. 'I don't know what you're talking about.'

'Don't you?' Bleakness invaded his expression. 'Then you're the first single female to cross my path lately who doesn't cherish such a notion.'

'There's a first time for everything,' she flared back, chin rising defiantly. 'I wouldn't consider you husband material if you were the last man on earth.'

Knowing what sort of husband he had been dragged the assertion out of her. At the same time her deeper instincts screamed a denial, as if there was another truth to be known here.

Intrigue sparked in the eyes fused with hers. His brows rose in an expression of ironic amusement. 'You wouldn't? Not even if I offered you marriage here and now?'

An infuriating glow flooded her features, and a tremor like an earthquake warning—but totally localised within her—threatened her mask of composure. There had to be an answer which wouldn't get her into more trouble than she was already. 'It's one way of getting a nanny to stay, I suppose,' she offered. Was she dousing the fire or adding fuel to it?

It was the right answer, she saw, with an outrushing breath of relief, as his grim features lightened fractionally. The relief was short-lived as his almost-smile impacted on her with all the warmth of a shark's jaws just before they closed over their victim.

'Clever,' he murmured. 'Of course there is a way to find out if you're telling the truth.'

'What's that?'

How stupid could a woman be and still function? The test he had in mind became startlingly evident as he closed the remaining gap between them and pulled her into his arms.

His touch was like fire as his fingers skimmed her nape. There was artistry in the way he moulded her head to receive his kiss, but by then the blood pounding at her temples and the tearaway rhythm of her heart were distracting her from the awareness that he was a little *too* expert at this.

Unable to control her response, she trembled, awaiting the touch of his lips which, when it came, was like wine. Sweet as honey, pure as flame, demanding and giving all at once. Playing with fire she might be, but there was an irresistible appeal in being swept along by a force as elemental as the one he awakened in her.

It was pure physical attraction, her brain insisted, but it was just as quickly silenced by more primitive responses which knew nothing of logic. No amount of reasoning could countermand the needs awakened by his touch.

No one had ever reached her on such an emotional level before. It was like everything she'd ever read about being made love to—everything she'd previously dismissed as exaggeration. If it went on forever, it would stop too soon.

'I rest my case.'

He might as well have poured cold water over her. The shock was comparable as he stepped away, a grim satisfaction in his steely gaze. Too late came the realisation that she had all but surrendered in his arms. No amount of protesting would override the physical evidence of laboured breathing, racing heartbeat and shining eyes—exactly as he'd intended.

Damage control was all Terise could hope to achieve now. 'So now you know. I chose you because you're wealthy, powerful—and eligible. Are you satisfied?'

He crossed to a bar and poured himself a generous measure of scotch whisky—the rarest brand, she noticed, with the heightened sensitivity which was becoming part and parcel of being around him. She gestured a refusal, being confused enough without adding alcohol to the matrix.

Resting his forearms on the bar, he skewered her with a sage look. 'If you knew as much about men as that statement is meant to suggest, you'd know better than to expect me to be satisfied with what is basically an aperitif to a much more stimulating banquet.' He sipped his drink, his gaze unwavering. 'You almost tempt me to show you the rest of the menu.'

There was no point asking for a drink now. It would only betray the dryness in her throat, further proving his point. 'I'm not h-hungry,' she managed.

'Then my demonstration has achieved its aim. We understand each other.'

Fury rose in her, displacing some of the shock which had held her in thrall. 'If you think I'm such a menace to your single status, why don't I leave now and be done with it?'

Her anger washed off him, leaving no trace. 'Because I want you here. You're the first person the twins have taken to since their mother died.' He gestured expressively. 'Don't think I haven't tried nannies before. I have. But the twins need more than well-meaning supervision. They need someone who understands them and can help them adjust to their loss.'

Before she could react he pressed on, 'What I don't need is an aspiring wife. That's the condition you'll accept in order to work for me. Understood?'

Even as she nodded compliance a deeper part of her argued that she would regret the bargain. It was absurd, of course. As the song said, a kiss was still a kiss. Just because it had shaken her to her foundations it didn't mean that she craved a repeat experience. This was the devil, she reminded herself.

So why was she having such trouble keeping it in mind?

Making the effort, she followed Ryan on a tour of the penthouse. It was huge and airy, the décor influenced by the blues and yellows of the French Impressionists—a surprise really, considering the austere elegance of the office floors below. Evidently some effort had been made to provide a cheerful city home for the children.

Terise's room was along a vast central hallway. The lush chalk-blue carpet and white furnishings had a friendly, provincial feel. An all-white bathroom opened off it.

Ryan opened a door at the far end. 'The twins sleep in here, so you'll be handy to them if they need you.'

In a room dominated by a wide, netting-swathed bed it was an effort, but Terise made herself sound businesslike. 'Where are the children now?'

'My housekeeper, Maggie Oken, is giving them dinner in the family-room. Afterwards you'll entertain them until their bedtime, then join me for dinner.'

Evidently he had no difficulty maintaining a businesslike distance. The thought was unexpectedly galling to her. Rather more waspishly than intended, she said, 'If I'm to be strictly an employee, is that appropriate?'

'Since I define "appropriate", it is. Unless you *do* have an ulterior motive?'

'Of course not. Should I dress for dinner?'

'We have no guests tonight, so you can please yourself.'

If that had truly been an option she would have been as far away from here as humanly possible. Instead she nodded acquiescence, explaining away her traitorous sense of anticipation as appreciation of having this chance to learn more about the children's background.

It couldn't have anything to do with the prospect of spending the evening with Ryan, she assured herself. Even the devil offered a higher price for a soul than one kiss.

CHAPTER THREE

THE size of the penthouse was a blessing. By the time Ryan had shown her around it Terise had regained most of her composure, so that her smile was warm and genuine when she was introduced to the housekeeper supervising the children's dinner.

Spoons poised in identical poses in mid-air, Trudy and Lisa looked wary as Ryan explained that Terise was their new nanny. 'Why can't Mrs Oken be our nanny?' Lisa asked truculently.

'We like her better,' Trudy chimed in.

So Lisa was the leader and Trudy the follower, Terise noted automatically. She waited to hear Ryan's response.

His tone dropped to a gentle baritone. 'What does Mrs Oken tell you when you come home from school?'

Tiny dimples cratered the small cheeks as the twins exchanged grins. '"Get out of my kitchen. The floor's just been washed",' they chorused, almost in unison.

Maggie Oken flushed at having her words recited back at her, but didn't contradict. Terise suppressed a smile.

'Isn't it better to have someone who isn't quite as busy as Mrs Oken with her floors—someone

43

who's waiting to play with you and look after you every day?'

At the word 'play' twin gleams sprang to cornflower eyes, and Lisa spoke for both children. 'It might be all right, I s'pose.'

Trudy nodded dumbly, and Terise released the breath she hadn't known she'd been holding. The twins were going to accept her after all. It was strange but it had already started to matter to her in a way she didn't care to examine too closely. She refused to think that it had anything to do with their father's disturbing effect on her.

Ryan dropped kisses on both golden heads. 'Finish your dinner, then you can show Terise your toys before bedtime.'

He led the way out of the room, gesturing for Terise to follow—which she did reluctantly. She would have preferred to use the informal mealtime setting to get to know the children better. She was also irritated by his imperiousness. He would have to be told that she didn't care to be snapped to attention with a gesture. But now wasn't the time to raise the issue. It would come when they were alone.

'Not in front of the children' was more than a phrase to her; it was an inviolable rule. As her father's only companion after her mother had died—until he remarried—she'd been involved in adult problems far more than was good for her. As a result, it was hard to recall a time when she'd felt truly carefree. She'd grown up vowing not to burden her own children with adult concerns before they were ready. She didn't have children of her own but she could see no reason to change her rule for those in her care.

It wasn't until she was seated in Ryan's study that she realised she hadn't thought about Clair in several hours. All her attention had been focused on Ryan and the children. As a measure of his ability to distract her, it reminded her to watch her step. It would be easy to forget why she was here.

A document slid across the desk to her, interrupting her reverie. 'I require your signature on this.'

Her gaze dropped to the printed document. 'What is it?'

'The standard contract I use for all my employees. It stipulates your salary and conditions, as well as my requirements—including a confidentiality clause between us.'

Her eyebrows lifted. 'A confidentiality clause? Surely my discretion goes without saying?'

His dark eyes hardened. 'Quite possibly, but I've found it's prudent to say it anyway. This way there's no room for misunderstandings later.'

'It's said that people suspect others of misdeeds they're inclined to do themselves,' she observed, then could have bitten her tongue off. The last thing she wanted to do was to alert him to her wish to avenge her step-sister.

His lip curled into a cynical twist. 'Do you have family secrets that I could spill to the media?'

It was so close to the truth that she felt the colour ebb from her face. She stifled an indrawn breath.

'Of course not.' The denial sounded shaky, even to her own ears.

'Then you have nothing to worry about, do you?' He pushed a gold-plated pen towards her.

Still she hesitated. The document bound her to a month's trial, after which she would be employed for a year under the terms set out in the contract. The trial was at his discretion, she noticed, annoyance flaring inside her. If he was unhappy with her performance he could release her at the end of the month. There was no such escape clause on her side.

'Shouldn't the trial period be mutual?' she asked in a low voice.

'I'm not the one on trial,' he countered. 'As a professional, you know what to expect from your duties. A month would reveal little more. On the other hand, I'm hiring an unknown quantity. Of course, it's unlikely that I would hold you here against your will.'

'Of course,' she murmured. But the decision would be up to him. The contract was specific and binding—but what choice did she have? This was her only chance to uncover some scandal she could use to hurt him. And, if she was honest, it allowed her to be close to the nieces who had already gone a long way towards winning her heart. With a heavy sigh she signed her name.

He looked satisfied as he retrieved the sheet and witnessed her signature. Then he rose and went to a liquor cabinet in one corner of the study. 'Shall we drink to your appointment?'

Now that the decision was irrevocable she had no reason to refuse. Drinking with him might enable her to get to know him a little better. 'All right,' she agreed.

As he poured cognac for them both her eyes were drawn to him as if by a magnet. His deft movements spoke of a self-confidence which fairly took her breath away. What must it be like to be so in command of any situation?

Not every situation, she remembered. There was still the mystery of his marriage, which she was determined to resolve. He might well be one of Australia's most powerful men, but she alone knew that he possessed a dark side which she planned to expose to the world if it was the last thing she did.

The thought that it might be—as it had been for Clair—made her shiver. Luckily Ryan blamed it on the sip of brandy she'd just taken.

'Easy with that stuff; it's potent,' he cautioned.

The brandy had plenty of company, she thought as the fiery liquid blazed a trail down her throat.

She had been wrong. Drinking with him felt far too intimate. Suddenly she was vibrantly aware of him, as if the switch from the business of the contract to the informality of the toast had also signalled a change inside her.

Like switching channels on a television set, she was suddenly receiving an entirely different picture. The aggressively efficient businessman had become a handsome, charming, intelligent and altogether too fascinating man, talking easily about his plans for the trade assembly.

Involuntarily she checked the level of the brandy in her glass. Almost untouched. There was only one other likely intoxicant in the room, and that was Ryan himself.

He noticed her hesitation. 'If you don't care for cognac I'll get you something else.'

Colour bloomed in her cheeks as she silently cursed his powers of observation. 'It's fine, thanks. I'm not much of a drinker.'

'An asset in your line of work, I'd think.'

'In what way?'

'Doesn't a childcare worker need nerves of steel and a certain amount of shockproofing?'

She gave a wan smile. 'I don't know about nerves of steel, but it does help to be relatively un-shockable when you work with small children.'

He answered her with a wry grin. 'I've noticed.'

'The twins?'

'Definitely. They almost gave their last nanny heart failure when they splashed tomato sauce over themselves and told her it was blood.'

It was original at least. 'Thanks for the warning.'

'Just making sure you know what you're getting into.'

As far as the twins were concerned, she had no doubts. Like all six-year-olds, they were a mixture of angel and devil—testing their boundaries at every opportunity. Their father worried her more. Did she really know what she was getting into with him?

He moved closer and she tensed reflexively, but he only removed the glass from her hand. The slight contact was enough to make her recoil as if stung.

'The twins will have finished their meal and will be expecting you. I have work to do before dinner.'

Annoyingly the dismissal rankled. She stood up with as much dignity as she could muster. 'Very well, then, I'll see you at dinner.'

His head was already bent over his paperwork when she let herself out.

What was the matter with her? she asked herself furiously. After the way she'd allowed him to mesmerise her, she should be grateful for the reprieve instead of feeling as hurt as a maiden scorned.

When he'd come towards her, for one insane moment she'd thought... No. She pushed the thought of herself in his embrace roughly from her mind, refusing to let herself be beguiled by his charm.

Forcing herself to recall what might lie beneath the charm, she recovered a little—enough to be in control of herself by the time the twins rocketed into the room.

A trace of chocolate ice-cream smeared the corner of Trudy's mouth, and Terise wiped it away with the clean handkerchief she carried for such purposes.

Trudy giggled. 'Mummy does that—only she uses the corner of her apron.'

'Mummy used to do it. She can't any more,' came Lisa's severe correction.

A quaver in the child's voice tugged at Terise. She dropped to her knees and gathered the children into her arms. 'You miss your mummy, don't you?'

'Yes.' Lisa's response was matter-of-fact. Trudy's was muffled, because her face was pressed against Terise's shoulder.

Her arms tightened around the children. 'Any time you want to talk about her, we can, you know.'

Trudy looked surprised. 'Can we? I thought we weren't s'posed to.'

Terise frowned. Was this the housekeeper's injunction or Ryan's? Either way, it wasn't good for the children. 'Some people think you'll feel bad if you talk about your mummy. But sometimes it hurts worse not to talk about her, doesn't it?'

Both children nodded solemnly. Suddenly shy, Lisa pulled away, and Trudy followed more slowly. The leader and the led. 'Daddy said you would play with us.'

Terise accepted the change of subject gracefully. She couldn't do more than leave the way open for them to express their feelings if they chose to. 'You'd better show me your toys and we'll choose a game before bedtime,' she said, injecting a cheerful note into her voice.

From a selection which would have done a toy shop proud, they chose a board-game whose objective seemed to be the devising of the most outrageous stories possible. Predictably, Lisa's attempts were the most fanciful, and calculated to impress Terise, but Trudy's showed surprising creativity.

The game not only occupied them until bathtime but also gave Terise valuable insight into the girls' different personalities.

Expecting groans of protest, she was surprised when they packed up the game and headed for the bathroom without complaint. Whispers came from the bathroom as they undressed.

Her suspicions aroused, Terise inspected the bathroom, but she could see nothing amiss as she filled the tub, adding pink bubble bath to make it more enticing. 'In you get.'

Submerged in the pink foam, the twins began to wash, but couldn't suppress their giggles. They were definitely up to something. 'Can I have the sponge, please, Terise?' Lisa asked around a giggle.

Lifting it, Terise gasped at the sight of a huge black spider crouched beneath it. The giggles intensified and she realised that she was being set up. At least it wasn't fake blood.

With a shudder of distaste she reached for the creature, which she could see now was quite obviously plastic. It was still more lifelike than she cared for, but she masked her reaction and stroked it with the back of a finger. 'Whose pet is this?'

The giggles became splutters of laughter. 'It isn't a pet—it's only pretend,' Lisa denied scornfully.

Trudy's eyes were round as saucers. 'Do you like spiders?'

'I can't say I *like* them—especially not inside the house—but most of them don't harm people. They're more scared of us than we are of them.'

The sound of muted applause greeted her response. She looked up to find Ryan lounging in the doorway leading to the children's room.

To her annoyance she became acutely conscious of the hair curling in damp tendrils around her face and the splashes of foam adorning her blouse, which steam from the bath had moulded to her figure. She had to fight not to drag a towel down to shield herself from his disturbing appraisal.

'Bravo,' he said softly. 'The last nanny screamed and flattened one of those before she realised it was plastic. These two thought it was better than television.'

She gritted her teeth and glanced at the children, who had become subdued since Ryan's appearance. 'Perhaps we could discuss this later?'

He inclined his head, but there was no acquiescence in his eyes, which shone with a fire she found altogether unnerving. Before she could decipher it, he straightened. 'As you wish. There is, however, one thing we'll discuss right now—and that's an apology from these two.'

He was making much more of the joke than it had warranted, undermining the fragile rapport she'd been establishing with the twins. But he was their father, and she was bound to comply with his wishes. 'If you think it's necessary.' Her tone said that she disagreed.

'I do.' He fixed the children with a stern look. 'How about it?'

Trudy looked down at the bubbles banked around her tiny body. 'I'm sorry, Terise.'

Lisa looked at her father. 'Sorry.'

'It's Terise you should apologise to—not me.'

'Oh, please...' Terise's plea escaped unbidden. Couldn't he see that the apology was less important than her need to make friends with the children?

His frown silenced her. 'Lisa?'

'Sorry, Terise.'

Satisfied, he spun on his heel, leaving them to finish the bath in sulky silence. Terise tried to cheer them up by singing an aboriginal lullaby. The strange words gained their interest, but the joy had gone out of the evening.

As she tucked them into bed they bid her a subdued goodnight, refusing a bedtime story. 'Maybe tomorrow night,' she said brightly, but her heart was heavy. All they'd done was act like the babies they were. No harm had been done.

Couldn't Ryan see that repressing their natural high spirits would do more harm than good in the long term? Surely her dignity didn't demand such a high price?

She was fuming by the time she'd changed into a black velvet evening skirt and an apple-green silk blouse which crossed over her breasts, emphasising her slight figure. It was a more feminine look than she wanted, for what promised to be a confrontation, but coming from the country she had a limited wardrobe.

Still damp from the bathroom, her taupe hair had sprung into a mass of thick curls and refused to be tamed. Like her temper, she thought, abandoning the attempt to restrain it. She had a feeling that Ryan wouldn't care to be kept waiting while she fussed with her hair.

He was already at the table and stood up when she entered, drawing a chair out for her. It was a long time since any man had been so solicitous of her—schools being equal opportunity places these days—and she was surprised to find the attention so enjoyable.

She had to remind herself that she was angry with him, especially when he insisted on studying her, feature by feature, with an appreciation that she found disconcerting.

'You look lovely, Terise,' he commented, pouring wine into a Baccarat goblet at her place.

'Thank you.' She took a sip of wine to still the tremor in her voice. 'However, I think you and I need to get a few things straight.'

His eyebrow lifted quizzically. 'You're offended because of a simple compliment?'

Warmth washed over her. 'Of course not. I'm offended because you interfered between the children and me this evening.'

His eyes glittered dangerously. '"Interfere" is a strange word to use, considering I am their father.'

'Perhaps "interfere" is the wrong word. Sabotage might be more appropriate.'

He had been slicing the smoked salmon entrée with the precision of a surgeon, but at her tone he looked up, his gaze icily direct. 'Go on. This should be interesting.'

What on earth had possessed her to use such a word? But it was too late now. She forced herself to meet his eyes without flinching, although her stomach lurched. 'I was getting on well with the twins until you cracked down on them for what was only a harmless prank.'

'It wouldn't have been so harmless if you'd suffered from arachnophobia, like their last nanny.'

She took a deep breath. 'Then she had no business being in this line of work. Teachers spend half their lives admiring the winged and crawling creatures the little ones bring them. To say nothing of those that have to be returned to the wild before they expire.'

A muscle worked in his jaw, as if he was restraining himself with an effort. 'Very commendable. No doubt your facility with insects will endear you to the children, but I don't see it as a licence for them to behave badly.'

'Neither do I,' she insisted, wondering where her courage was coming from. It would have been much easier to give in to him. But Ryan struck her as a man whose respect needed to be earned. The only question was, could she afford the price? 'I'll talk to them about practical jokes at a more appropriate time and in an appropriate way. They're only six years old.'

He ate in silence for a few seconds. 'So all your sympathy is with the twins?'

'My concern is for the twins,' she amended, on a rising note of desperation.

He pushed his plate aside and planted both palms flat against the table. 'I hired you for your expertise with children, but understand this: I won't have you siding with the children against me.'

Dismay widened her eyes. 'You're their father. I wouldn't dream of coming between you and the twins.'

'Their mother did—all too frequently.'

His clipped tone couldn't take the sting out of his words. Had Clair really been capable of such behaviour? Her letters had suggested that Ryan came between *her* and the children. Caught between Ryan's blunt assertion and what Terise herself thought that she knew, she was rendered speechless.

'You seem shocked,' he went on relentlessly. 'I don't suppose someone with your tender heart can imagine a woman using her children as weapons to get her own way.'

If it was true, she had only one possible answer. 'You're right. I can't.'

A challenge glittered in his eyes as his gaze impaled her across the table. 'Then I can count on you to restrain yourself from criticising my actions in future?'

Her chin lifted. 'Not where the children's welfare is concerned,' she denied. 'As a matter of fact——'

His explosive sigh cut her off. 'For a moment I actually thought you might manage to keep your opinions to yourself.'

She tossed her napkin on to the table and pushed her chair back. 'If that's what you want, you should let your chauffeur continue minding the children. I'm sure Marcus has no idea how they should be brought up—which should suit you to a T.'

Before she could leave the table, his hand clamped around her wrist, the pressure forcing her back into her seat. 'For such a little thing, you have quite a temper,' he observed, wry humour lightening his tone.

Acutely conscious of the strong fingers encircling her wrist, she made herself remain still. Unfortunately she had little control over the nerve impulses which jumped the length of her arm in response to his touch. 'In the first place, I'm average height. You're the one who's ridiculously tall.'

'True—such things are relative,' he drawled. 'And in the second place?'

'In the second place... Darn it, there *is* no second place. You're right. I have no business telling you how to bring up your children.' Her lashes dropped, veiling her swimming eyes. 'It's a bad habit of mine. I'm surprised my former boss didn't warn you.'

His look became speculative. 'She had nothing but praise for your skills, although she did mention that you never back away from a fight where a child's welfare is involved.'

'Well, now you know it's true—but it doesn't mean I'm always right,' she admitted, dredging the confession from the depths of her soul.

His index finger made a circular motion across the pulse point at her wrist, as if he was measuring the beat, although he seemed barely aware that his hand still rested there. Unfortunately her pulsebeat was well aware of the fact, and responded accordingly.

'In this case, I'll admit you have a point,' he said softly.

The admission so startled her that her lashes fluttered over her astonished gaze. 'You will?'

'I'm well aware that the trade assembly bid is taking a lot of my time. If it wasn't a temporary thing, I'd be more concerned, but I've been telling myself the children will benefit in the long run. But when you're six years old, even six months must seem like an eternity.'

'Especially when your father is all you've got,' she added in a strained whisper.

He removed his hand slowly, almost with reluctance—which must have been her imagination. Steepling his fingers in front of himself on the table, he said, 'What is your expert solution?'

'There isn't an easy one,' she admitted, noting the weariness in his eyes. 'You have heavy responsibilities—to your employees and their families as well as to your own family. But it would help if you could spend a little more time with Trudy and Lisa. Seeing them only after school at your office is positively Victorian. Don't you go on family picnics or outings together?'

'We used to,' he supplied in a clipped tone, which warned her that she was trespassing on dangerous ground.

She had a sudden uncomfortable vision of Ryan and Clair sharing a picnic rug while the two golden-haired toddlers played around their feet.

A tightness around her heart threatened her composure, but she resisted it. He had been married after all. Family gatherings were to be expected. 'You stopped taking the children out after your wife died?' she asked, her throat closing with emotion.

He reached for his wine glass, cupping it between strong hands. His knuckles whitened, threatening to snap the stem. But his control was absolute enough to ensure that he did not. 'Not that it's any of your business, Terise,' he said coldly, 'but the family outings stopped well before my wife died. She didn't enjoy them so there was no point.'

His head lifted and the brilliance in his eyes seared her. 'You seem to be unusually curious about my relationship with my late wife, so let's get something clear from the outset. Your job is to care for the children. The rest of my life doesn't concern you. Understood?'

What would he have said if he'd known that his life *did* concern her—because getting revenge for Clair was still uppermost in her mind. But he didn't deserve any forewarning, so she kept her head high and met his look squarely as she said, 'I understand perfectly.'

CHAPTER FOUR

USED to a hectic teaching schedule, Terise found her new job left her with almost too much time on her hands. The twins were at school for half of each day. Looking after their needs and shopping for them rarely filled the hours until it was time to collect them.

In desperation she volunteered to help Maggie Oken with some of her duties. The housekeeper was grateful—both for the help and for Terise's company.

'Normally we'd have a caterer for tomorrow's dinner party, but thanks to you helping with the preparations I can handle it splendidly,' she confided as they worked side by side in the well-appointed kitchen.

'It's such a small party—only five people,' Terise commented. 'I'm not sure if I'm expected to participate.'

'You are—Mr Westmore told me this morning,' Maggie informed her. 'Better wear something smart. The guest of honour is a delegate from the world trade assembly.'

Terise nodded. 'So I understand. I'd better go shopping before I pick up the children. Do you have any suggestions on shops I could try?'

The housekeeper eyed her enviously. 'I know where I shop. But with your figure you could go to any designer in Sydney.'

Terise laughed. 'I may have the figure, but not the budget, I'm afraid.'

'In that case you'd do well to check out some of the factory outlets in the inner city. A smart shopper can pick up a designer dress for a song.'

Terise filed the information in her head. It was just what she would do. As well as the all-important delegate who had a vote in securing Sydney as the site of the world trade assembly, the guests at tomorrow's dinner party were executives from Ryan's organisation. If she must attend, Terise wanted to look the part. Luckily her first fortnight's salary was already in the bank. Her living expenses were almost non-existent, so she could afford to splash out on some new clothes.

'Thanks, Maggie,' she said sincerely. 'This job wouldn't be nearly so enjoyable without your company.'

A faint tinge of red coloured the other woman's cheeks. 'It's a nice change to have another woman around for me too,' she confided. 'I've been on my own here for years.'

The housekeeper had been in Ryan's employ for even longer than Marcus, Terise recalled. 'Wasn't Mrs Westmore company for you?' she asked in surprise.

The housekeeper sniffed, and wiped floury hands on a towel before reaching for the kettle. 'She was fine as long as I remembered I was only an employee. You'd have thought she was a duchess or something.'

'But Clair wasn't like that,' Terise blurted out before she could stop herself. 'I mean, I knew her before her marriage, and she didn't seem stuck up at all.'

'Then you didn't know her very well. Once she had her hands on Mr Westmore's money she thought it put her above everyone else. Oh, she was happy enough when she was out socialising, and she loved shopping, but she'd never ask me for the time of day—let alone advice on anything.'

A leaden sensation invaded Terise. She knew she should put a stop to this conversation—especially as it was obvious that the housekeeper hadn't liked Clair and it was colouring her judgement. But there was no other way to get at the truth. 'She was a good mother, though,' she said, in a carefully neutral tone.

'She was a wonderful mother,' Maggie admitted, but Terise's relief was short-lived. 'She loved the twins as babies, billing and cooing in their cots. But once they were old enough to get into scrapes and demand her attention she lost interest in motherhood.'

'Yet the children still miss her terribly.'

'I don't doubt it. I've heard that children can ask to go back to a bad home because it's all they know. Trudy and Lisa probably think all mothers were like theirs. If you ask me——'

'*Did* you ask her, Terise?'

The male voice cut across the conversation like a whipcrack, silencing Maggie and spinning Terise around with shock. Ryan filled the doorway, his grey eyes burning with an anger more fierce than any she'd ever seen. Shaken, she weighed her answer. Dissembling would bring his wrath down on Maggie, whose only crime was satisfying Terise's curiosity. 'Yes, I asked her,' she whispered.

'We were both gossiping, Mr Westmore,' Maggie insisted, her face pale. 'It was thoughtless—but harmless, surely?'

His face tightened into a remorseless mask. 'Gossip is seldom harmless. Especially when the subject can no longer defend herself.'

'You're right, of course.'

'Then we understand each other, Maggie.' He turned to Terise, his expression glacial. 'In my study, Terise. Now. We have some talking to do.'

She knew who would do the talking, and she could hardly blame him for being angry. As he saw it, his marriage was not a topic for casual conversation. But it didn't stop her own anger from flaring.

More than ever she wanted to know what had gone on between Clair and Ryan. Why had Maggie's description been so unflattering? Had Clair become a different person as the wife of a wealthy man? Or had the marriage simply brought out traits which Terise was unwilling to acknowledge?

What was Ryan's role in all this?

Her back rigid with tension, she followed him to his study, seating herself in a chair before he could arraign her in front of his desk like a recalcitrant school-child. In her teaching career she'd used the same psychology herself, and she refused to let him try it on her.

To her mild surprise he sat down opposite her, rather than taking a position of power behind the vast desk. Seated, he was still a good head taller, but she lifted her chin to meet his angry expression.

'What the hell did you mean by that little scene?'

She schooled her voice to calmness. 'Exactly what Maggie told you. We were simply gossiping.'

'In clear contravention of my express wishes?'

'Your express wish was that I concern myself with the welfare of the children. I can't do it unless I know more of their background—which includes their relationship with their mother. I can hardly pretend she didn't exist, can I?'

Ryan regarded her pensively, one eyebrow lifting. '*Were* you seeking background for the children's sake?'

She refused to take the coward's way out. 'Not this time.'

Some of the tension seeped out of him. 'I can't damn you for your honesty, although I won't condone your behaviour. But I take your point about the children's background. From now on any information you require is to come from me. I trust that's clear enough to prevent any further misunderstandings?'

Her breath escaped in a hissing sigh. 'Yes, it's clear enough.' At the same time her heart sank. She could hardly expect honest answers from him to the questions she needed to ask. Such as why Clair had been so unhappy, until she had left in desperation, only to lose control of her car less than an hour away from Ryan's Bowral home.

'Is there anything you particularly wish to know?' he asked, his voice impressively steady, although she had a good idea of the extent to which he must be bracing himself.

He was hardly likely to tell her anything she could use against him, she thought, uncomfortably aware of a sudden reluctance to probe what were obviously sensitive areas—even though it was the reason she'd taken this job. So she asked instead about the children. How they had coped with their loss. How Ryan had helped them handle their grief.

It was difficult to harden her heart against the torment she heard in his answers. She found herself aching to tear down the wall around his emotions, distantly aware that her concern wasn't exclusively for the children. What was going on here?

'If that's all, I'll get back to work.' The discussion was clearly at an end.

She stood up. 'Would you mind me taking some time off this afternoon to go shopping? I need some new clothes for the dinner party tomorrow.'

He frowned. 'Your schedule is your own affair, once the twins' needs are met. But there's an easier solution closer to hand.'

Her brows drew together in puzzlement. 'What kind of solution?'

'My wife's clothes were given to charity, but there were several designer outfits on order, which arrived some time afterwards, and I've done nothing about them. If they're to your liking, you may as well have them.'

A lump swelled in her throat. 'I don't think...' He had been furious to catch her gossiping about his marriage. Now he was prepared to give her clothes designed for his late wife. Was it an olive branch, now that the dressing down was over? The man was bewilderingly complex.

He gestured impatiently. 'It's up to you. But the clothes are brand new—not even unpacked. It makes more sense for you to have them than to let them go to waste. Come, I'll show you.'

He opened a door off the study into his private apartment. There was a ballroom-sized bedroom, with French doors opening on to a sunny glass-roofed terrace. It would be an inviting place to enjoy breakfast, she thought.

Beyond the bedroom, a luxurious marble-tiled bathroom was visible through a half-open door. Beside it was another door, which Ryan flung wide to reveal a walk-in wardrobe. Most of the contents were masculine, but one side held dress bags clustered together. He swept them off the rack and carried them to the bedroom, where he spread them on the bed.

'Choose anything you like. I'll have Maggie send the rest to charity,' he said, with a dispassion she could hardly credit him with feeling.

He propped himself against the doorframe while she gingerly unzipped the first bag. Her gasp of admiration was involuntary. 'It's beautiful.'

The dress was a fully lined Chanel shirtmaker, in a soft cream wool with dramatic black trimming and signature gold buttons. She set it carefully aside and opened the next bag. Swathed in tissue wrapping was a fluidly draping suit of fine jersey, carrying an Italian designer label. Clair certainly hadn't stinted herself.

The last garment eclipsed them both, she saw as she held up a bewitching cocktail dress in superbly draping black velvet. Tiny diamonds studding the low neckline were the only adornment. She had little doubt that they were real.

She looked questioningly at Ryan. They were all so lovely, yet she felt like a usurper even handling them. 'Try the Chanel first,' he instructed, his eyes unreadable.

Suddenly shy, she ducked her head. 'Now?'

'You can use my dressing-room.'

With the door closed between them, she tried the dress on, telling herself that it was no more than a working uniform, to enable her to fit in with his business guests. Yet she was achingly conscious of him, separated from her by the flimsiest of barriers. Her fingers were clumsy as she fastened the gold buttons.

The dress fitted perfectly, skimming the gentle curves of her hips in flattering style. The buttons ended just above the knee, leaving a slit of fabric to open provocatively with every move.

Ryan's inspection seemed as impersonal as a doctor's, until she caught sight of something burning in his eyes. Was he regretting offering her the dress? The thought sent a wave of pain surging through Terise. 'This isn't going to work,' she said as her eyes started to blur.

He regarded her with hard intensity, the burning fading—or had she imagined it in the first place? 'You're right. The black is more your style.'

One of them had misread the other. Still, it was easier to carry the black velvet dress into the dressing-room than to argue a point she wasn't sure she had any right to question.

It took her only a moment to change. As soon as the velvet—soft as a kitten's fur—settled over her body, she knew that this was the dress. The gently puffed sleeves tapered to narrow wrists and the slightest of ruching edged a deep V-yoke, making her look incredibly fragile and—dared she think it?—beautiful. At least she *felt* beautiful, and it was an almost magical experience. Clair had been the family beauty. Could her mantle pass to Terise with a dress?

The look on Ryan's face when she emerged told her that it was just possible. In fact it was more than a possibility, she realised, catching her breath. No man had ever looked at her with such undisguised admiration.

Surely it couldn't be desire that she read in the taut lines of his face and the bunched muscles at his jaw? Terise was the schoolmarm—the bookish one. Looks such as the one on his face weren't directed at her. At least they hadn't been until now.

He moved closer, his hand lifting to brush a strand of hair away from her face. At the feather-light contact fire tore along her veins. Before she could organise her chaotic thoughts, he stepped away. 'The dress is yours.'

She wanted it more than she had ever wanted any other garment in her life—if only for the way it made Ryan look at her. But conscience was stronger. 'It's lovely but I can't take it.'

His eyes became hooded. 'Then I'll tell Maggie to burn it.'

Her reaction was involuntary, the words almost leaping from her throat. 'You can't—it would be a crime.'

'A greater crime to let someone else wear it after you,' he said, in a husky baritone which stripped her nerve-endings raw.

She had no doubt that he would carry out his vow if she continued to refuse the dress. It wasn't as if it had ever belonged to Clair, she told herself, knowing that the battle was already lost. 'Very well, I'll wear it—but only for the dinner party,' she conceded.

He made a dismissive gesture, as if her reasoning was of no consequence to him. His mask of non-emotion was firmly back in place. 'Take them all.

There will be other occasions when you'll need to be suitably dressed.'

Only the certainty that he would destroy the lovely garments if she refused made her gather them up. 'As you wish.'

She had no intentions of wearing them for anything other than official engagements. Letting Ryan provide clothes for her formed no part of her battle plans—even if she had weakened momentarily at his reaction to her in them.

It had been surprise, nothing more, she told herself. It wasn't as if she wanted him to look at her so...so possessively. Not until she knew for sure what manner of man she was dealing with.

Her obvious confusion seemed to amuse him, and a mocking smile played around the corners of his mouth as she escaped with the clothes. He probably thought he had her measure already, she thought furiously. He had yet to find out what manner of woman *he* was dealing with.

When he left his apologies that he wouldn't join her for dinner, she told herself that she didn't care—and part of her accepted it as true. The part that didn't troubled her all through the evening, although she tried to be cheerful for the children's sake—joining them for dinner and games before bedtime, which had become their routine.

Maggie was friendly but distant—probably still upset over Ryan's censure earlier in the day—and Terise felt very much alone by the time she retired to her own bed.

What was she going to do? The housekeeper
hadn't told her anything she could use against Ryan.
In fact, she had made it look as if Clair had been
at fault. Terise might have known Ryan's staff
would be on his side.

Her own observations of him were equally un-
helpful. The newspapers could hardly make much
scandal out of a hard-working family man. Her
mouth twisted ruefully. Was she going to have to
plant a tape recorder in his study to gather evidence
against him?

She hadn't expected it to be this hard. Didn't
every corporate giant have skeletons somewhere in
his closet? Unless . . . She pushed away the thought
that there might be nothing to find. Clair's experience hadn't been nothing. Terise would just
have to keep her eyes and ears open until she found
something—anything—she could use to tarnish that
perfect public image of his.

Next day was Saturday, and Terise had planned to
take the children on a picnic, leaving the way clear
for Maggie to prepare for the dinner party that
evening.

The car was waiting for them when they reached
the underground car park. Terise was laden with
the children's things, and a picnic basket prepared
by Maggie. By the time she had stowed everything
into the car the twins were fastening their seat
belts and jiggling up and down with impatience
to be off.

But there was a surprise in store when the driver's door opened, and instead of Ryan's chauffeur his place was taken by Ryan himself.

The girls squealed with delight, but Terise felt a chill trickle down her spine. Perhaps he was only seeing them off. Surely he didn't intend to spend the day with them?

'You recommended I spend more time with the children,' he reminded her when she voiced the question a little shakily.

Of all times, why had he picked now to listen to her? 'I thought you disapproved of me interfering.'

He gunned the powerful motor. 'I still do, but sometimes even unpalatable opinions contain a grain of wisdom. Are you telling me now that it isn't a good idea?'

It wasn't, but for other reasons. After yesterday, when she had reacted to him so unexpectedly, the last thing she needed was a whole day in his company. But there was nothing she could do about it. 'Of course you should spend time with your children,' she said, her voice barely above a whisper. She reached for the door handle. 'I assume you'd rather have them to yourself.'

His hand closed over hers, steel against satin. 'You assume wrong. As your boss, I'm ordering you to accompany us and—enjoy yourself.'

He could order the one but not the other, she thought mutinously, but settled back in the padded leather seat.

He drove well, she noticed unwillingly as they joined the flow of traffic over the Harbour Bridge and through the busy northern suburbs which led to Ashton Park—a lovely wild reserve on the harbour foreshores below Taronga Zoo. Terise had discovered it soon after arriving in Sydney, and had thought it must look the way all Sydney must have looked when the area had first been settled in 1788. It was an ideal spot for a family picnic.

Except that they weren't a family, she reminded herself. On such a glorious day, in such scenic surroundings, she could easily have forgotten this vital fact.

Ryan acted more like a solicitous husband— making sure the bushwalk they tackled after leaving the car wasn't too much for her, and taking her elbow to help her clamber over rocks around the foreshores.

The children raced ahead, swarming over the rocks and stopping to examine the tiny creatures they spotted in pools left by the receding tide. Ryan cautioned them against venturing too far ahead, but Terise still spent far more time alone with him than she would have preferred. She tried to tell herself that the prickles of excitement gripping her were caused by the simple pleasures of the outing.

She had almost made herself believe it by the time Ryan rounded up the girls, announcing that it was time to head back to the car for lunch.

'It seems Maggie has excelled herself,' Ryan observed as Terise set out chicken roulade, salads and crusty bread rolls. Dessert consisted of fresh fruit and slices of Maggie's chocolate mud cake, with a flask of coffee for Ryan and Terise.

'All we need is a jug of wine,' she mused, after polishing off a surprising amount of lunch.

He tilted a dark eyebrow at her. '"And Thou beside me singing in the Wilderness"?'

Her nervous laugh disguised the sudden warmth which had pervaded her at his words. 'I doubt if the poet had twin six-year-olds in mind when he wrote that.'

'If not then, in the future,' he said, his meaning unmistakable.

Terise's cheeks grew warm and she looked away, ostensibly to check on the twins. Curled up on the rug, they were asleep like puppies sharing a basket. Her heart began to melt.

'Attractive, aren't they?' Ryan's voice was husky.

'Yes.' The lump in her throat permitted no elaboration.

Before she knew what was happening he had slid closer on the rug, until their thighs touched. His hand cupped her chin and turned her until her mouth was aligned with his. Her breath became shallow as she realised that he meant to kiss her.

She felt her pulses gather speed. As surely as she knew her own name she knew that she wasn't going to refuse him, although instinct warned her that she should. Ever since he had first kissed her every part of her had craved a repeat performance, had hungered for it as a thirsty person craved water.

What had he done to bedevil her so?

Then he did kiss her, his hand curling around the nape of her neck to deepen the pressure. Her senses began to spin as her softness yielded to his hardness, with a sense almost of homecoming. For whole, dizzying moments, she managed to forget who and what he was. There was only a heady sense of rightness, of completeness as he wove a magical spell of sensation around her, drawing her deeper and deeper into the web of his embrace.

Trudy rolled over and began to rub her eyes, making a mewing sound like a baby animal. The sound was slight, almost lost in the rhythms of the bush and the seashore, but it was enough to make Ryan draw back. He took his time, seemingly unperturbed that his daughter might see him kissing the nanny.

'Incredibly attractive,' he murmured, his eyes molten as they lingered on her dazed expression.

She had to know. 'Why did you do that?'

'Can't you guess?'

'But you told me... You warned me...'

'I warned you against looking for anything permanent from me. A kiss is hardly a lifetime commitment.'

She felt as if he had dashed cold water over her. So she was simply another of the day's pleasures—there for the taking. She could hardly believe she had been such a fool.

What was worse, he must know exactly how foolish she had been. He must read it in her eyes and the flushed excitement in her face, to say nothing of the trembling which betrayed her as she gathered up the picnic things. She shouldn't be surprised by his behaviour. Clair had given her enough warning. She had no one to blame but herself that she had ignored it.

'There is such a thing as sexual harassment,' she reminded him angrily, knowing how far away from any such thing his kiss had been.

'What's 'rassment?' Lisa demanded, sitting up.

He folded his arms across his broad chest, a challenge gleaming in the grey eyes. 'Yes, Terise, do explain it to us.'

'You know perfectly well what it is—as you've just demonstrated,' she hissed.

'Oh, but that hardly fits the category, since harassment——' his explanation was pointedly aimed at Lisa '—is when you bother somebody when they don't want to be bothered.'

'Like when I ask you things when you're working?' Lisa interpreted.

'Exactly.' His gaze raked over Terise, daring her to contradict him. 'When you want to be bothered, and you show it, it's something else entirely.'

His meaning was all too clear. By inviting his kiss, and returning it, she had lost all claim to outrage. It didn't prevent her from feeling utterly miserable, knowing that she'd betrayed her quest as well as herself.

To make matters worse, the kiss haunted her all the way home, and she saw from the taunting glances he threw her way that he was well aware of it.

She was thankful that the children, tired after the outing, had settled down with picture books in the back seat. Being alone with her thoughts wasn't comfortable, but it was better than enduring Ryan's verbal sparring, where she invariably came out the loser.

She was startled enough to jump when his low voice intruded on her reverie. 'I'm going away next week. It's another reason I wanted to spend today with the children.'

Her sense of loss caught her by surprise. How could she feel the loss of something that wasn't hers in the first place? Since a response seemed expected, she asked, 'Where are you going?'

'To my property in Bowral. The trade assembly delegate and I have a lot to discuss, and the country atmosphere will set the scene.'

Will win the delegate's vote for Sydney, she interpreted. Unreasoning anger rose inside her. 'Can't you take Trudy and Lisa with you? You saw how much they enjoyed your company today.'

'This is a business trip,' he reminded her curtly, evidently less than pleased with her suggestion.

She persisted, aware of the anxiety the children would suffer if he went away without them. They were bound to associate his departure with the loss of their mother, and she said so.

He gave an impatient sigh. 'You have a point, unfortunately. And it is school holidays next week, so there's no real reason why they shouldn't come along. You'd have charge of them while I'm working.' He fell silent, considering the idea, then added, 'Maybe a glimpse of family life might help the cause.'

Terise felt the slow burn rising. 'Naturally the bid is what matters.'

'Shouldn't it?' His voice was arctic.

'You know the saying about all work and no play.'

'It hasn't made me dull company so far—as you found out for yourself today.'

She turned her face aside, to hide her heightened colour, and was relieved to see that they were turning into the underground car park. It saved her from answering the unanswerable yet again.

She almost wished she hadn't suggested taking the children with him, because she had just sentenced herself to more time in his company when it was the last thing she needed. It was right for the children, but knowing that didn't help her own misgivings.

At least he would be occupied with the trade delegate, she consoled herself, noting the black bulk of an Alpha Romeo in the visitor's spot next to Ryan's reserved parking space. How much trouble could she get into with another businessman there to act as chaperon?

CHAPTER FIVE

TROUBLE came in many guises, Terise was reminded when she joined Ryan in the living room for pre-dinner drinks with his guests.

He stood shoulder to shoulder with two formally dressed men, one of whom must have been the delegate. Both men paled into insignificance beside the awesome sense of presence she was beginning to associate with Ryan. He also wore formal dress, of herringbone double breasted jacket with a black satin collar over a white dress shirt and silk bow tie, but he wore it with a style the other men lacked. He might have been commander of a battleship, or president of a country. It was all suggested in the commanding poise of his stance.

When she hovered on the threshold, he set his drink aside and came towards her. 'Come and meet the delegate.' He took her arm, and some of his confidence flowed into her as if she had been transfused. She held herself straighter, curious to see which of the men he would nominate.

But he ignored them both, steering her to a chair whose back was to the door. 'Cecily Elbrun, I'd like to introduce one of my staff—Terise O'Neill.'

The woman rose in a fluid movement which suggested she might once have trained as a dancer. 'How do you do, Miss O'Neill?'

Stunned into silence, Terise brushed the fine-boned hand which was held out to her. She could hardly believe that this petite, exquisitely turned out woman was a delegate to the international trade assembly. The look she flashed at Ryan said that he might have warned her.

The amusement sparking in his eyes told her that he was enjoying her startled reaction. Cecily Elbrun was no more than thirty, as slender as a porcelain doll and with a sweet face that hinted at a fascinating ancestry. Hair the colour of midnight cascaded to her waist, barely tamed by a pearl ornament at her nape.

'It's a pleasure to meet you,' Terise finally managed to stammer. She was eternally thankful not to have rejected the velvet dress, which she now wore with black satin shoes and the diamond ear-studs she had inherited from her mother. No doubt Cecily Elbrun could calculate the value of her outfit to the last dollar. Thanks to Ryan, Terise's clothes, at least, wouldn't be found wanting.

The other two men turned out to be members of Ryan's board of directors. Terise now knew why she had been invited—to balance the numbers of men and women.

Ryan himself seemed to lose interest in her once the introductions were out of the way, preferring to direct his notice to the lovely delegate, who seemed more than willing to bask in his undivided attention.

For some reason Terise found herself bristling as she watched them together, the fine hairs on the back of her neck lifting whenever Cecily Elbrun touched his sleeve to make a point. It wasn't as if she cared, Terise assured herself. Even though Ryan had kissed her that same afternoon, he'd made it clear that it meant nothing. Business before pleasure, she thought, wondering acidly if he was combining business *with* pleasure this evening.

Maybe that was why he'd resisted taking the children to Bowral with him. This looked like the kind of lobbying he would relish.

She comforted herself by thinking that he was probably showing his true colours at last. Was there a scandal in his relationship with Cecily Elbrun which Terise could leak to the Press?

The possibility should have excited her. It was why she'd taken this job after all. So why did she feel so uncomfortable, trying to eavesdrop on his conversations with the other woman? What was happening to her desire for revenge for Clair's sake? The question troubled Terise so much that she finally gave up, and turned her attention to the executives seated on either side of her at dinner.

From them she learned that Cecily Elbrun had been born in Vietnam to French parents, spending most of her youth travelling with her family. Now she lived in Australia, her time taken up with more travel on behalf of the world trade assembly.

No wonder Ryan found her fascinating, she thought, unwillingly comparing the other woman's glamorous background with her own country-town upbringing. Why it should matter, she wasn't sure, but it hurt all the same.

'You made quite a hit with Alex and Gordon,' Ryan told her after dinner. Cecily had returned to her city hotel, prompting the executives to take their leave also.

'They're charming company,' she said, unable to keep a barbed note out of her voice.

'Like our delegate. What do you think of the lovely Cecily?'

It was impossible to deny. 'She *is* lovely. You seem to have made . . . quite a hit with her yourself.' She threw his own words back at him with the slightest touch of irony.

His silence was electric as he regarded her speculatively. 'You don't like her?'

How could she admit that she didn't like what Ryan became with her? It was the man Terise had come to find, yet, having found him, she didn't like it one bit. The only puzzle was why it should trouble her so much.

'I hardly know her,' she said lightly. 'From Alex and Gordon I gather she has a reputation as a tough negotiator in business.'

'And the appearance of being anything but, which serves her well.' He poured a nightcap for them both without consulting her. As she accepted the drink, he added, 'I've known Cecily a long time—since we were teenagers. Both of our parents were in the diplomatic corps, so we've knocked around the world together for years.'

Again a feeling very like jealousy flooded through Terise, but she resisted it. What he did and with whom was none of her business—except when it helped to solve the riddle of his relationship with her stepsister. In his company, and with the late hour cloaking them in intimacy, it was dangerously easy to forget.

'Won't your friendship create a conflict of interest when she has to vote on Sydney hosting the assembly?' she asked, anxious to keep the conversation on neutral ground.

'Cecily is experienced enough to separate the two.' He gave a cynical laugh. 'So you can forget what you're thinking, about me taking her to Bowral to seduce her into supporting our bid.'

Her face betrayed her shock. It was so exactly what she *had* been thinking that she was stunned. Could he read her mind now? 'It's hardly any of my business, is it?' she demanded, uncomfortably aware of how waspish she sounded.

'Agreed.' He snapped the word out. 'But since you seem to enjoy—gossip—I thought it worth stating for the record.'

Terise felt a chill fist close around her heart. This was the man in Clair's letters—the tough, unfeeling cynic, who spoke of seduction so casually. Nothing he said should surprise her, yet she couldn't suppress an anguished pang that he thought so little of her. It didn't make any sense.

'That was a mistake,' she said with quiet dignity, refusing to let him see how his words had wounded her. 'I assure you it won't happen again.'

He finished his drink. 'Then I shan't refer to it again. Goodnight, Terise.'

'Goodnight.'

Slowly, thoughtfully, she followed him out of the living-room, turning off lights as she went. The trail of darkness behind her found an echo in her thoughts, which were as bleak and dark as an abyss. She kept seeing Ryan with Cecily, the other woman's hand on his arm in casual intimacy. No matter how hard she tried to tell herself that this was the real Ryan Westmore, she couldn't make herself accept it.

She knew why.

Part of her wanted to believe that the charming family man who had kissed her so persuasively this afternoon was the real Ryan Westmore.

She went to sleep in a ferment of confusion over the puzzle. Maybe the time spent at Bowral would resolve the question once and for all.

In their excitement, Trudy and Lisa became almost impossibly naughty in the days before the trip. When they tore through the apartment the day before their departure, squealing and shouting, Ryan stepped out of his study. 'Is this a sample of what I'm in for when we get to the property?'

At the sight of him Terise bit back the sympathy which welled inside her. He'd worked until well past midnight the night before, and his eyes were rimmed with shadows. He'd missed dinner the previous evening too, preferring to have a tray sent to his study.

But none of it was the children's fault, which was all that should concern her. 'They're only excited,' she explained. 'Once we're in the country they'll have room to run around and work off their high spirits.'

His lids lowered over blazing eyes. 'That sounds dangerously like a criticism to me, Terise.'

She was tempted to snap that he could take it as he liked, her own nerves also being stretched to the limit by the confinement of the apartment. However spacious, it still lacked open air and greenery, which she found she needed as much as the children did. Parks were a poor substitute.

'I'm sorry if it sounds like criticism,' she said sincerely, 'but it's the truth. Six-year-olds need room to run and play.'

He threaded long fingers through his charcoal hair. It was amazing how the cant of one eyebrow could reveal his displeasure more than most people's rages, she thought, bracing herself. But all he said was, 'Then it's as well we're leaving tomorrow. Are the children ready?'

She had anticipated his wishes correctly. 'I've done most of their packing. We can leave whenever you wish.'

He nodded tautly. 'Two o'clock tomorrow, then. Marcus will drive you and the children. I'll drive Cecily in her car.'

Remembering the black Alpha Romeo, Terise wondered how Cecily had persuaded him to chauffeur her. She couldn't imagine that it was due to any limitations on Cecily's part. If she was playing the helpless female, it was for her own reasons. It was hard to imagine anyone less potentially helpless.

She kept her thoughts to herself and went to round up the children. Perhaps the news would calm them down before they incurred more of their father's wrath.

Ryan and Cecily had already left by the time Terise and the children were ready. At the last moment Trudy had announced that she was missing her favourite stuffed toy—a bear called Morton—without whom she refused to close her eyes at night. They couldn't leave until the bear had been restored to its tearful owner.

'Are you sure that's everything?' Terise asked, her voice slightly ragged.

Trudy gave her a wide-eyed look. 'We couldn't leave Morton behind, could we?'

It was a look to melt stone. Probably genetic, Terise thought as she ruffled the golden hair. 'Of course not. Let's go, then. Your father will be wondering where we are.'

Unless he was too busy playing host to the lovely Cecily, she thought, her errant mind conjuring up an image of his long-fingered hands resting capably on the steering-wheel of the powerful car. For a crazy moment she also saw herself beside him, her hair ruffled in the breeze from the sun-roof. His hair would be feathered across his wide forehead, making him look more dashing than usual, as light and shade played across the rugged planes and angles of his face.

Flushing, she drove the image from her mind, replacing it with the more likely one of Cecily

laughing up at him as they reminisced about
growing up in diplomatic circles. Ryan would be
driving with the effortless skill Terise had observed
on the way to Ashton Park—no doubt with a hand
free to reach for his companion.

Stop it, she told herself furiously. Neither image
was necessarily accurate—especially not the fantasy
of herself and Ryan together. It could never
happen—even assuming that she was foolish
enough to want it. She knew what marriage to him
had done to Clair. Wasn't she, Terise, supposed to
be the clever one? Hadn't her stepmother said many
times that what Clair had achieved with her looks
Terise would have to achieve with her brains?

Well, thinking about him in those terms was
hardly using her brains. An involuntary tightening
within her body was enough to remind her that it
wasn't her intellect he appealed to. His attraction
was much more primitive, and its power was almost
frightening to one used to thinking her way through
life.

It was just as well Marcus was driving, she
thought as they set off. Threading her way through
the maze of her thoughts was bad enough, without
having to deal with the city traffic as well.

The expressways were clearer, and they reached
the southern highlands in under two hours, which
allowed for a stop for the twins to have a snack
and stretch their legs.

On the road again, Terise set them to watching
for the turn-off to Westmoreland—Ryan's eighteen-
hectare property. Marcus knew the way, of course,

but it helped to keep the increasingly restless
youngsters occupied.

'There it is! There it is!' screamed Lisa, beating
her twin by seconds.

Trudy tugged at her arm. 'Look, there are
Daddy's cows.'

Marcus swung the car along an avenue of elms
through which she glimpsed black and white cows
grazing in velvet paddocks. A mob of kangaroos
rested in the shade of a giant eucalyptus, their sleepy
eyes barely registering the car's passing.

The house was set atop a knoll of natural
bushland against a backdrop of densely forested
mountain ranges. The style was federation, down
to the leadlight windows and the wide verandas
roofed with bullnosed corrugated iron. Set on
Wollombi sandstone foundations, the house looked
as if it had been standing there for a century.

Marcus informed her that it had, having started
life as a staging post for Cobb and Co coaches. An
old-fashioned garden of agapanthus, climbing roses
and peppercorn trees fairly invited exploration.

Terise began to feel as excited as her charges, until
a glimpse of a black car in the circular driveway
dampened her spirits. Telling herself that it was
foolish to resent Cecily's presence didn't help.
Knowing that the other woman was already here
made her feel as if a shadow had slid across the
sun.

Freed from the confines of the car, Trudy and
Lisa burst into the house like bullets fired from a

gun, their aim straight and true as they homed in on their father in the living-room.

Recalling his previous resentment at being disturbed by them, Terise followed more sedately, ready to whisk them away if Ryan objected. To her surprise he scooped up a daughter in each arm and held them high. 'How're my best girls? Enjoy the drive?'

'It was fun. Terise bought us ice-cream in Berrima,' Trudy confided.

His eyes sparkled as his glance included her in the charmed circle. 'Did she, now? What kind?'

Lisa touched his nose and giggled as he pretended to bite her finger. 'You know I always have chocolate.'

'And I always have strawberry.' Trudy was missing a front tooth so it came out 'thtwabewwy'. Ryan laughed and nibbled her finger too, before setting them down.

Terise watched him in amazement. Was this the same fiercely preoccupied man who'd almost bitten her head off in Sydney for letting the twins run around the apartment? Surely the country air hadn't affected him so quickly? Then she had it. Cecily must have worked some magic on him during the drive. The thought was unexpectedly distressing, try as she might to tell herself that she welcomed the change.

'How was your trip?' she asked, striving to sound conversational and almost succeeding.

'Pleasant. Cecily's gone to her room to make some business calls before dinner.'

It hardly sounded relaxing to Terise, but to another workaholic it was probably normal. She gathered up the twins with a gesture. 'I'll get these two settled in. Marcus showed me where their rooms are.'

'Yours is alongside, with Cecily and I across the hall,' he explained. 'You'll want to be near the girls.'

It wasn't a question. And she didn't need to ask whether he wanted to be that close to Cecily. It seemed as if Ryan had everything worked out.

Other than at mealtimes, she saw little of him over the next couple of days. Cecily was also absent, she noticed. Well, they had come here to work— although Terise doubted whether the trade assembly took up every moment of their time together. At the thought, desolation swept through her. It happened altogether too often lately. Here, she didn't even have Maggie to talk to and the twins—delightful as they were—were hardly stimulating company.

She was returning from putting them to bed one night, when she quite literally collided with Ryan in the hallway. The hands he put out to steady her burned like brands through her T-shirt. 'Where are you off to in such a hurry?' he asked, amusement colouring his voice.

Why did he always manage to make her feel no older than the twins? For a fleeting moment she wished she was wearing something more glamorous than the T-shirt and jeans in which she'd been riding with the children. Her hair was tied back with a scarf, from which dozens of tendrils had escaped to curl around her face.

'I was going to shower and change then have an early night,' she said, disturbingly aware of his closeness. He was so big and the hall so narrow that she would have to force her way past him to escape.

Under his scrutiny she felt herself colour, but she forced herself to meet his gaze without flinching. 'I was hoping you'd join us for dinner. You are entitled to some time to yourself, you know.'

He had already informed her that the couple who looked after the property were more than happy to take Trudy and Lisa off her hands for a few hours whenever she felt the need. The couple had known the children since birth, and regarded them as part of their own family. From what Terise had seen, the twins more than returned their affection.

'I'll remember,' she said stiffly, unhappy with the way her senses had suddenly gone on red alert. His touch on her arm was light and completely impersonal, but her skin reacted to it as if to a caress. Prickles of awareness travelled along her jawline to connect with the nerves of her shoulders and spine. Heat spilled along her entire body until a tremor shook her.

What was it about this man? It couldn't be simple good looks. Terise had known handsome men before. Teachers—especially presentable young single ones—had ample opportunity to meet their opposite numbers, usually other teachers or single parents of their pupils. So dates had never been a problem. But never before had Terise been so mesmerised by a man.

Was it his air of absolute self-assurance, reflected in the manner and stride which said he owned whatever land he walked over? Or was it the sheer force of a personality which drew eyes and interest wherever he went? Terise had heard the term 'alpha male' many times, but had never seen anyone who personified it so totally.

Releasing the breath she'd been unaware of holding, she managed a cool nod. 'Dinner would be nice—if you're sure I'm not intruding.'

Puzzlement momentarily darkened his features. 'Intruding? Of course not. What makes you think you could be?'

It was almost painful to admit it. 'You and Cecily have a lot to...discuss.' Among other things—none of which concerned the hired help.

He laughed explosively. 'Don't you think three days of business talks is enough? Weren't you the one who accused me of too much work and not enough play?'

Her mouth twitched in an unwilling smile. 'It was hardly an accusation. And you did your best to set me straight on that score, if you recall?'

'Oh, I recall very well. I also recall exactly how I set about it.'

Her breathing became tight suddenly as his arm slid down the wall to trap her between it and his body. The hall seemed even narrower as he cupped the side of her face, stroking it gently until it was all she could do not to press her lips into his open palm. The memory of his last kiss lingered on her lips and in her mind like a brand, so she could barely tell if this was an echo or if Ryan was really kissing her again.

The warm, demanding feel of his mouth shaping hers brought her to her senses. It was real, and this time there was no excuse. Cecily was here in the house, and Terise was poaching on territory not only forbidden but dangerous in the extreme.

Butterflies dipped and soared in her stomach and she clung to him dizzily, aware of every corded muscle under her fingers. Like the victim of a stage hypnotist, she knew perfectly well that she shouldn't be letting him do this—and went ahead and let him do it anyway.

The tap of heels on the polished tallow wood floor penetrated the mist swirling around her. Ryan drew back lazily, much less concerned than Terise. In fact, amusement sparkled in the eyes he brushed briefly over her before he turned to greet Cecily.

'I've convinced Terise to join us for dinner.'

The other woman's blue eyes were less welcoming. 'Really? I thought we still had a lot to discuss.'

'A fresh point of view always helps,' he said, his glance flicking back to where Terise stood, mortified, against the panelled wall. 'Later, then.'

His brisk stride took him past both women to his own room. Cecily looked after him, her mouth set in a grim line. 'So you're his fresh point of view, are you?'

'He didn't mean that the way it sounded,' Terise tried.

Cecily gave a hollow laugh. 'Ryan never says anything he doesn't mean.' Her eyes narrowed. 'If you don't know that yet, perhaps you don't know him too well after all.'

Horribly uncomfortable, Terise felt bound to re-assure the other woman. 'Actually, I don't. I've only worked for him for a few weeks. I gather you've known him a great deal longer.'

'As he's probably told you, our fathers were in the diplomatic corps. His father was a full am-bassador. Mine drank rather too much to rise that high. But he did well enough, and drinking is an occupational hazard in diplomacy. So Ryan and I spent a lot of time together when we were young. Since I went into international trade relations we've stayed close. We understand each other.'

'You love him?' Terise could have bitten her tongue out for voicing the question, but it was out before she could stop herself.

Cecily looked startled, as if the question hadn't occurred to her. 'I suppose so. There aren't many men like him. But he's always been there for me and I assumed he always would be.'

In Cecily's shoes, Terise knew that she wouldn't have made such a dangerous assumption. Men like Ryan *were* rare, and even more rarely available, without some fatal flaw to explain their status. Ac-cording to Clair's letters, Ryan *did* possess a fatal flaw. Maybe this was what had kept Cecily from deepening their relationship, since she knew him so well.

Without betraying her relationship to Clair, Terise could hardly voice her suspicions. In any case, Cecily seemed capable of taking care of herself. 'I'd better get ready for dinner.'

Cecily seemed to return from a great distance. 'I suppose you'd better, since Ryan is your employer. We're dining at eight. He doesn't like to be kept waiting.'

She turned on her heel, leaving Terise bristling with annoyance. Cecily had been perfectly correct to remind her of her place in Ryan's life, but it still rankled.

She had more than a suspicion that Ryan had only kissed her to make Cecily jealous, perhaps intending to force her hand. The other woman's reaction when Terise had asked if she loved Ryan served to make Terise think that Ryan's tactic—if it was indeed a tactic—was working. Cecily had looked like a sleepwalker awakening at long last.

Dinner was as much of an ordeal as Terise had expected. Cecily had changed into a stunning halter dress in fuchsia satin, which revealed gleaming shoulders and a swanlike neck in perfect diminutive proportions. Beside her, even in the Chanel dress, Terise felt ungainly—although she had actually lost weight since coming to work for Ryan.

She couldn't help noticing how adroitly Cecily played on her size, emphasising Ryan's masculinity by contrast. It was guaranteed to flatter any man, and Ryan looked as if he was enjoying the sport.

To his credit, he refused to let Cecily talk business all evening, and drew Terise into the conversation whenever she tried to fade into the background. It was more attention than she wanted, and his speculative look suggested that he was aware of her attempt but was determined not to let her get away with it.

If his aim was to make Cecily jealous, he was succeeding, she noticed uneasily. Until now Cecily had considered Terise beneath her notice. Now she seemed constrained to outshine Terise—which wasn't difficult, with her knowledge of languages and a wider world than Terise had ever known.

At the coffee stage she rested her chin on one hand, smiling at Terise. 'Ryan's taking me bushwalking tomorrow. I've seen so much of the world and so little of my own back yard that I can't wait.'

Swallowing a lump which had wedged itself in her throat, Terise forced a smile. 'How nice. I thought of taking the children on a picnic.'

'Then we'll combine the two,' Ryan announced. 'It's time I saw something of Trudy and Lisa.'

Cecily looked put out. 'Surely a bushwalk is too strenuous for the little ones.'

They were likely to leave Cecily standing, if she but knew it, but Terise kept silent, hoping that Ryan would take the hint and let them go their own way. She didn't care to spend a whole day playing gooseberry in any case. 'We'll be fine on our picnic,' she insisted.

A frown darkened Ryan's features. 'No doubt you would. But, as their father, I've made my decision.'

'In that case, Terise should come along to take care of the children,' Cecily conceded, a smile hovering around her mouth without reaching her eyes.

'Terise was invited on her own merits. It's time she had a day off. I'm sure you and I can handle two six-year-olds between us.'

Terise looked from Ryan's set face to Cecily's barely concealed dismay. What was Ryan up to? Was he trying Cecily out as mother material? The thought sent a tremor of reaction through Terise until she caught herself. It was only logical, if he was considering a future with Cecily, that his children should get to know her.

Somehow, the thought gave Terise little comfort.

CHAPTER SIX

TERISE stared out of the bedroom window in dismay. The weather in the southern highlands was notoriously unreliable. Why couldn't it have rained today, instead of dawning sunny and clear?

She sighed. There was to be no escaping Ryan's plans for the day. They would all go bushwalking together, one big, happy family. She wasn't even on duty today, able to hide behind her responsibilities to Trudy and Lisa.

The pity of it was that under other circumstances she would have adored bushwalking in the beautiful highlands. It was the company which didn't appeal to her. Cecily had made it plain that she didn't want Terise along, so she was unlikely to be pleasant company. It promised to be a long day.

So she was pleasantly surprised when Cecily greeted her warmly when she joined the others for breakfast. The other woman even helped Trudy and Lisa with their breakfasts, Terise noted in surprise. Cecily was taking seriously Ryan's injunction that it was to be Terise's day off.

She was also demonstrating her suitability as a mother, Terise noticed with a twinge of dismay. Her reaction troubled her—particularly the sense of possessiveness which ripped through her at the sight of Cecily tending to the twins.

By the time they set off she had the beginnings of a tension headache, and could only hope that the fresh mountain air would clear it.

They were heading for Mount Gibralter, known locally as the Gib, a famous landmark between Mittagong and Bowral. Rising almost nine hundred metres, it was known for its walking tracks and look-outs ranged around the rim of the old volcanic peak.

Marcus dropped them off along a reservoir service road off the Old Bowral Road. 'We walk from here,' Ryan told the excited six-year-olds.

Terise regarded the start of the service road with some misgivings. 'Maybe Cecily's right. This looks awfully steep.'

'It's all right, only the first kilometre or so to Mittagong Look-out is uphill,' he assured her.

There was nothing for it but to shoulder the light day-pack he handed her and follow him. Cecily shepherded the children ahead of her, until they were between her and Ryan, with Terise in the rear. She told herself that it was the headache making her feel so stupidly sorry for herself.

'Enjoying the walk?' She started when Ryan appeared at her elbow. She hadn't noticed him slipping back until he was level with her as they followed a spur crest towards the first look-out.

'It's beautiful,' she admitted, gesturing towards the distant views of the western gorges and mountains.

'It occurred to me that I might owe you an apology,' he said, drawing a look of surprise. 'I did rather hijack your plans for today.'

Was he regretting bringing her along, when he would rather have had Cecily to himself? 'It's no problem,' she said with forced lightness. 'The children are having a wonderful time.'

'After being confined to a city apartment?'

She lowered her head. 'I had no right to criticise your lifestyle.'

'No, but you did it anyway.' He touched a finger to her chin, lifting her head to meet his eyes. 'And I have the feeling you'll do it again if you see the need.'

At his satisfied grin, she felt answering sparks leap into her eyes. 'No doubt—if only to give you a change from all those yes-men in your organisation.'

A devilish smile was his response. 'So you think I keep yes-men on my team?'

Recoiling in mock-horror, she lifted her hands palms upward. 'Of course not. I'm sure they say no when the boss does.'

His compelling grey eyes narrowed warningly. 'How long is it since somebody turned you over their knees?'

'Oh, not since I started taking self-defence classes,' she snapped back, concerned with the turn the conversation seemed to be taking. Sparring with her when Cecily was only a few metres away was in the poorest possible taste, and Terise was annoyed with herself for responding.

A single line of irritation angled across his brow. 'You have no need of self-defence around me, Terise.'

Oh, no? What she really needed around him when he was this close was a four-metre-high barbed wire fence—preferably electrified for good measure. Dressed for hiking, in moleskins, denim shirt with the sleeves rolled back and a bushman's hat resting far back on his head, he looked infinitely more dangerous than in a suit and tie.

The outdoor clothes emphasised his hawklike demeanour, making him appear fitter and leaner than usual. Sunlight glowed in a band across his charcoal hair, giving it an almost metallic gleam. It was tempting to reach up and brush back the strands straying across his wide forehead.

Her throat dried. 'No?'

He drew a heavy breath. 'No. I may have a reputation for toughness in business, but it doesn't extend to my treatment of women and never has.'

Not even with Clair? she wanted to ask. His electric gaze was so forthright that Clair's letters might have been describing another man entirely. Unless . . .

Terise drove down the thought that she could be falling under his spell. She was certainly in danger of losing her objectivity. The thought made her pick up her pace. 'The children are getting too far ahead.'

His hand grasped her elbow, forcing her to stop. 'Cecily's with them. They'll wait for us at the look-out. First, I want to know what's eating you.'

Panic coiled through her, although she managed to keep most of it off her face. Did he suspect who she was? 'Why do you ask?' she stammered.

'The way you look at me with those haunted eyes, as if you're waiting for me to turn into a monster. I thought it was because I ruined your plans for today, but if that's not the answer, what is?'

It was so close to the truth that she felt herself going white. She *was* waiting for him to turn into the monster of Clair's letters. But the longer she waited, the less likely it seemed. Or else she was already so far under his spell that she could no longer see him as he really was. It was a possibility which hadn't occurred to her when she'd hatched her scheme to discredit him. Now, even if she found something incriminating about him—and it seemed increasingly unlikely—would she have the will to use it?

'I don't know what you mean,' she whispered, aware that she was betraying herself with every sharply drawn breath.

One eyebrow canted accusingly. 'No, Terise? When we first met, I suspected you of having a hidden agenda. I thought you might be angling for marriage, but you denied it. But *something's* on your mind, and I intend to find out what it is.'

She jerked her head towards the look-out. 'We should go on. Cecily's waiting.'

A light glinted in his smoky gaze. 'Is Cecily the problem, Terise?'

No, she wouldn't allow herself to think so—far less have him suspect it. She managed a defiant toss of her head, angling her hair to conceal the flush which rose to her cheeks. 'She will be unless we get up there.'

He bit off a sound which might have been an expletive, and picked up his pace, forging a path to the look-out with a speed which sent stones showering past her. The twins attached themselves to each arm and towed him towards the look-out.

Behind him, Cecily watched, a satisfied smile on her delicate features. She had evidently noticed the alacrity with which he had rejoined her, and had put her own interpretation on it.

Despite the beauty of the walk, the day was ruined for Terise from that moment. She had done the right thing, urging him to rejoin Cecily, but she had a hard time making herself believe it. There was still a feeling of wrongness about the situation, as if she had completely misread it in some important way.

Fortunately the children's chatter masked her withdrawal as they picnicked in a forested glade in the former volcanic crater. She was aware of Ryan's eyes on her, as if they were laser beams searing her skin, but he left her alone and she tried to tell herself that she was glad.

Trudy and Lisa's feet were starting to drag by the time they headed down a steep section of track towards a farm, where Ryan had arranged for Marcus to meet them with the car.

Surrogate motherhood had lost its appeal for Cecily, too, and Terise was once more in charge of the twins. She didn't mind. Their chatter helped to keep her mind off Ryan, striding ahead of her as if the walk was just starting instead of almost over. Where did he get his boundless energy?

'Look, Terise. Look where Lisa is.'

Following Trudy's outstretched arm, Terise felt her heart leap into her mouth. While she had been distracted with Trudy, Lisa had slipped ahead. Spotting an echidna halfway down a steep bank, she had climbed down to investigate. One slip and she could tumble all the way down the mountain.

'Lisa, hold tight to that tree beside you,' Terise instructed, draining all fear from her voice so as not to alarm the child.

Lisa looked up, her tiny face strained. 'I'm stuck. I can't get back up.'

Dropping to her knees beside Trudy, Terise said softly, 'Very carefully run ahead and bring Daddy back here.' As soon as the child had moved off, Terise cinched her lower lip between her teeth and began to inch her way down towards Lisa. 'Here's my hand, darling. Reach as far as you can, but don't let go of the tree with your other hand until I tell you.'

She almost wept with relief when the tiny hand curled around hers. Anchoring herself to a tree with her free hand, she began to pull the little girl up. 'You can let go now, Lisa, I've got you.'

Her palm was red-raw from gripping the branch by the time Lisa was close enough to grab. Suddenly the child's weight was taken as Ryan lifted her clear. He set her safely on the path above.

'Don't move an inch, young lady. I'm going to get Terise.'

Determined not to wait for him, Terise began to climb the slope under her own power, but the bank had been eroded by water and gave under her before she reached the top.

With lightning speed Ryan snatched at her hand, saving her from going over the embankment, but she felt her ankle twist awkwardly under her.

Although she bit back her cry of pain, she only half succeeded. Ryan abandoned all caution and hurtled down the bank in a shower of stones. Bracing himself against a tree, he gathered her into his arms. 'I'm all right,' she insisted.

His mouth was set into a grim line. He looked like a human gauntlet—beyond argument, even if she'd had the strength. 'I'm carrying you up.'

The heat from his broad chest radiated through her as he hooked an arm around her body and another under her knees, carefully keeping her injured ankle clear as he lifted her up the steep slope. Compared to Cecily, she must be a leaden weight, but he gave no sign of it, transferring her to the safety of the track as if she were no heavier than Lisa or Trudy.

When she went to unfasten her boot, he stayed her hand. 'Better leave it on for now. The boot will control any swelling until I can get you to a doctor.'

Feeling foolish, she shook her head. 'It's nothing serious. If you help me I'm sure I can walk back to the car.'

'You're going to need all those self-defence lessons if you expect me to let you try.'

'But you can't carry me.'

'Can't I?'

Before she could utter another word she was back in his arms, all resistance crushed by the force of his hold on her. At his instigation the twins attached themselves to Cecily, who followed them down the remaining distance to the paddock where Marcus was waiting.

Soon afterwards Marcus took Cecily and the twins home while Ryan waited with Terise in the rooms of a medical specialist, who had opened his surgery at Ryan's instigation especially to treat her.

Ryan maintained a brooding silence as they waited for the results of her X-rays. Probably furious with her for spoiling an otherwise perfect day. 'I'm sorry about this.' She gestured towards her leg, elevated on the examining-table.

Ryan swore caustically. 'You can hardly be sorry for saving Lisa from a bad fall. What I want to know is why you had to go down there yourself. I was only metres ahead of you on the track.'

At his furious tone she lowered her head, his anger paining her more acutely than the ache in her ankle. 'I didn't want to startle Lisa by calling out.'

'So you decided to risk your own neck. Don't you realise you could have been killed?'

She kept her features rigid, absorbing his anger. It was probably a reaction to seeing his daughter in danger, and had nothing to do with Terise herself. She was relieved when the doctor rejoined them, clipping her X-rays to a light board and studying them with professional detachment.

Ryan moved to stand at the man's shoulder, his eyes assessing the films. 'Nothing broken, thank heaven.'

The doctor nodded. 'I didn't think so, but I wanted to check for hairline fractures. If you keep her off that foot for a day or so, she'll be fine. I'll give you some painkillers she should take to get a good night's rest.'

Terise felt an almost irresistible urge to call out, 'Hey, I'm over here.' It was her ankle, but the doctor had acted as if the problem was Ryan's.

She soon found out why. 'I'll send your wife some crutches, so she can move about without putting any weight on the ankle. But she should stay off it as much as possible.'

She waited for Ryan to correct the doctor's assumption but he merely nodded and said, 'Fine. I'll see she follows your orders.'

They left, with Terise managing awkwardly on the crutches and wishing she could wave a magic wand to make her ankle carry her away as far and as fast as possible. Hearing her name coupled with his had caused a reaction every bit as exquisitely painful as the one in her foot.

She'd hated being linked with him, she tried to tell herself, but had to quell a suspicion that she was being less than honest with herself.

All was quiet when the taxi Ryan had arranged dropped them back at Westmoreland. Ryan had spoken to the children by mobile phone, arranging for them to spend the night with the caretakers, Kate and Patrick, by the same means. The couple adored the twins, and were only too pleased to have them for the night.

'I feel terrible about this. Kate and Patrick shouldn't have to do my job,' she grumbled, more to herself than at anyone.

'They'd be offended to hear it called a job,' he pointed out as he helped her into the house and settled her on a couch in the living-room. 'They see themselves as unofficial grandparents.'

All the same she felt useless. If only she hadn't been so stubbornly determined to climb up the bank by herself, she wouldn't be in this fix. 'At least let me prepare some dinner,' she volunteered. 'I can do it on crutches well enough.'

'You'll do no such thing.' His tone brooked no argument. 'The crutches are for essential movements only. That doesn't include waiting on me.'

'What about Cecily?' She couldn't imagine the delegate being too pleased at having to prepare her own meal.

'Cecily's on her way back to Sydney. With you injured she thought things might become difficult, so she decided it was better if she left.'

He didn't sound pleased about it, Terise thought abjectly, reading her own interpretation into his chill monotone. 'This won't affect her vote on the Sydney bid, will it?' she ventured, horrified to think that her stubborn pride might have undermined his hard work.

His jaw clenched. 'At this moment I couldn't give a damn about the vote.'

He sounded as if he meant it, and she sighed inwardly. If he wasn't worried about Cecily's vote, it must be the woman herself he missed. Terise couldn't imagine anything else which would have stirred such intense anger. 'She didn't have to leave because of me. I'd have been fine resting in my room.'

'The fact remains that she *has* left, and hiding yourself away won't change anything. So why don't you stop trying to take the blame for all the world's ills and let someone else take care of *you* for a change?'

She didn't have much choice. But misery gnawed at her as she suffered him making a bed around her on the couch. Every movement caused her ankle to bark a protest, but she maintained a tense silence, determined to cause him no more problems.

Moments later he was back, with a glass of water and one of the doctor's painkillers. 'Did you think I wouldn't notice?' he asked softly, in response to her questioning glance.

His troubled, half angry expression made her wish he was less perceptive, but arguing would only annoy him more, so she swallowed the capsule with the water. 'Thank you.'

Of course he was angry with her, she thought, hearing him moving around the kitchen. Despite his assurance that Cecily's vote wasn't an issue, Terise couldn't help worrying about the delegate's abrupt departure. Terise's presence on the bushwalk had annoyed her to begin with. The accident had probably been the last straw.

Knowing he would stand over her until she did so, Terise ate a little of the pasta dish Ryan brought to her for dinner, but the painkillers had made her eyes heavy. She was asleep before he took the tray away.

In her dream she saw Ryan and herself on the bushwalk, but this time there were two Ryans. One was charming and thoughtful. The other was cruelly demanding, urging her to keep up whenever her pace lagged.

When she felt her self slip and tumble down an embankment she was caught in strong arms, knowing without looking that they belonged to the charming Ryan. The other watched her from the trail, his expression unyielding. He had his arm around a woman who looked like Cecily Elbrun.

The savage sensation which tore through her as she looked up at them caught her off guard. Then she looked at the arms cradling her and found that they were the branches of a eucalyptus tree. Ryan and Cecily were walking off arm in arm, leaving her alone.

She felt herself start to slip and tensed, aware of the sharp drop below her. She jolted awake to find herself on the couch in the shadowy living-room.

Lord, what a dream. She stirred, trying to shake it off, and gasped as a thick jolt of pain washed up her leg from her ankle. Biting down on her lip prevented the cry from escaping, or so she had thought.

She became aware that she wasn't alone in the room as a dark figure shifted in an armchair opposite her. 'Ankle hurting?'

'A little.' In truth, it was a mass of pain, which radiated along her calf with every movement. While she slept the muscles had cramped, and the urge to move to ease them warred with the protests from her ankle every time she did so.

He came over to her, snapping on a lamp which bathed them both in golden light. 'I can imagine. Unfortunately it's too soon to give you another painkiller.'

'It's all right.' She became aware that it was dark outside. 'How long have you been sitting there?'

'A few hours.'

She tried to struggle upright. 'There's no need. Honestly, I'm fine. You should get some rest.'

His hand on her shoulder eased her back against the pillows. 'I am getting some rest.'

'I mean in your own bed.'

'Only if you agree to join me.'

Her eyes snapped wide. 'What?'

'I stayed because I wasn't sure I'd hear you if you called out. But if you came to bed with me it would solve the whole problem.'

And she had a good idea of how many new ones it would create. Heat flooded through her at the very idea. 'In your dreams,' she said defensively.

The lamplight washed metallic highlights into his hair, but the glint in his eyes was all his own work. 'How did you guess?'

She turned her face away, glad of the dim light to hide the consternation she could feel in her expression. This wasn't the conversation they were supposed to be having.

He dragged his chair closer to her. 'Since you won't come to bed with me, I'll keep you company. We've got all night, so you can tell me your life story.'

This was the last thing she wanted to do. 'It's pretty boring,' she dissembled.

He folded his arms across his broad chest. 'I don't bore easily. Tell me how you got into teaching, for starters. Were you a straight-A student?'

It was so wide of the mark that she choked back a laugh. 'Lord, no. I was the class black sheep. I didn't settle down to serious study until my teens.'

'You—a black sheep? It's hard to imagine.'

Because she was a prim, proper schoolmarm now? 'It's true,' she insisted. 'I hated school. I was the only kid in my class without a mother, and I played up to show I didn't need one.'

He steepled his hands in front of himself. 'You lost your mother when you were young?'

'When I was seven. I missed her dreadfully, although Dad did his best to be both mother and father to me. We were good friends right up until he died. I still miss him.'

There was a slight pause. 'Your father never remarried?'

Alarm bells went off in Terise's head, boiling away the dreamy intimacy of the last few moments. This was dangerous territory, but Ryan was waiting for her answer. 'Yes,' she admitted reluctantly. 'Dad married the teacher who called him in to discuss my bad behaviour—so you could say I brought them together. After Dad died my stepmother moved back to Sydney. We're still friends.'

Before he could probe further she tried for a change of subject. 'Cecily tells me your father was an ambassador. You must have lived in some fascinating places.'

His scowl told her that the tactic had worked. 'And some hell-holes.'

'I beg your pardon?'

His face was blank, his back rigid. 'Diplomats don't always get a choice as to where they're posted.'

'Is that why you didn't become a diplomat yourself?'

His jaw tightened. 'There are several reasons. For one, I'm not nearly diplomatic enough.'

'Oh, but——'

'Don't pretend you haven't noticed,' he cut in. 'I have no time for the niceties of diplomacy, preferring to get straight to the point of any argument.'

It explained why he was so successful in the cut-throat world of big business, she thought. 'Isn't the trade assembly bid a diplomatic exercise?' she couldn't help asking.

He frowned. 'Yes, if you mean the kind where the main language spoken is money. This bid is all about how many billions of dollars the host city is prepared to spend to make the trade assembly a success. Fortunately the city also benefits handsomely. But it's more a question of economics than diplomacy.'

It fitted her preconception of him as a hard-nosed cynic whose main concern was the bottom line, but again she found herself resisting it. Her sense of confusion deepened.

Perhaps learning more about his background would help. 'Is your father still an ambassador?' she pressed.

He shook his head. 'He died a few years ago. It was in all the newspapers.'

Memory returned to her, and with it a coldness like icy fingers caressing her spine. His father had been Grant Westmore, the diplomat who had been kidnapped and held hostage for five years in the Middle East. Her heart went out to Ryan. How had he endured the torment of wondering whether his father was alive or dead?

Her fingers grazed her lower lip. 'I'm sorry. I didn't realise.'

'It isn't something I advertise,' he said, shadows shifting in his eyes. There was more pain here than he permitted to reach the surface.

Was this what had built the wall around his emotions? Maybe even turned him into the monster of Clair's letters? If so it might be explainable, if not excusable. 'What happened?' she asked.

'He was returned to the family but his health never recovered. He took up a desk job in Canberra but died a few years later.'

'You loved him.' It wasn't a question. Despite his veneer of cynicism, she sensed the reality underneath, wondering at the same time when she had begun to read him well enough to be so sure.

His eyelids lowered momentarily. 'He was my father.'

'And your mother?'

'She lives on a property she inherited from her family in England. We've never been close but I see her whenever I go over there.' His eyes narrowed. 'Hell of a family, aren't we? Not quite your image of Papa Bear, Mama Bear and Baby Bear?'

'Teachers deal with all kinds of families. I learned long ago not to expect fairy tale set-ups.'

'Even in your own family?'

Her hollow laugh was involuntary. 'Especially not in my own.'

'Yet you avoid talking about them.' When she started to protest, his look silenced her. 'When we started, you soon switched the subject to my family.'

'Only because there isn't much to tell.'

'You're a liar,' he said, so softly that her head came up, her eyes as startled as a fawn's.

'What?'

'There's a lot more to you than meets the eye,' he said, in the same deceptively mild tone—although she heard the steel underneath. 'I'm well aware that our meeting wasn't accidental, and I don't buy that bull about you coming to me for a job,' he continued, overriding her attempt at denial.

'Then why did you hire me?'

'Because you're good at what you do. I also prefer you where I can keep an eye on you. You're up to something, and I intend to find out what it is.'

CHAPTER SEVEN

THE silence lengthened uncomfortably. She couldn't deny his accusation because it was true. Right now she would have given a lot for it to have been otherwise. Hearing him talk about his father, sharing his tragic memories, had disturbed her.

She didn't want to picture him shouldering the burdens of his family while waiting for news of his father. It subtly altered her perspective—like meeting an enemy and finding out that he was as human as herself. She tried to shake off the feeling but it persisted.

With it came another uncomfortable possibility. Could Ryan himself be getting in the way? He attracted her in a way no man had done before, but that didn't mean... No. She couldn't be falling in love with him.

'No!' The word was wrenched from her, the gesture of denial so forceful that her calf muscles pulled on her injured ankle. She swallowed a cry as pain jolted along her leg.

Nevertheless Ryan heard her, and was beside her in an instant, gathering her into his arms to rock her gently. 'Go ahead—yell if you want to. It will probably help.'

Aware of the warmth of his arms around her, she shook her head. 'I'm fine.'

He frowned. 'So I see. Where did you learn to be such a stoic?'

His comment provoked a slight smile. 'I'm not, really. You should see me when I go to the dentist.'

He gave a mirthless laugh. 'Would you believe, me too?'

Her eyes widened. It was impossible to imagine Ryan having any fears at all. He had called her a stoic, but he was the rock of Gibralter—the alpha male.

He *was* teasing her, she realised as the skin around his eyes crinkled and a warning light flashed in the grey depths. 'I don't believe you,' she denied.

'OK, maybe I exaggerated—but you must admit it took your mind off your pain.'

It had done much more, she realised, becoming aware of a new kind of ache settling around the region of her heart. He held her tightly enough for her to feel his long fingers splayed hotly across her back. Her breathing quickened as he brought one hand around to caress the line of her jaw.

Unconsciously she tilted her head back, the gesture answered by his sharp intake of breath. She opened her eyes to find him watching her, his taut features hinting at an internal battle with himself.

'Ryan?' she said uncertainly.

She watched his jaw knot, then he leaned over her, his mouth finding hers with the precision of a heat-seeking missile.

Pleasure swelled through her, the sensation so bittersweet that it was only a heartbeat away from pain. Her first instinct was to resist, but the noble intention was almost instantly swamped by a wave of pure ecstasy.

An unbearable hunger swept through her. With trembling hands she reached up to touch the side of his face, half convinced that she was dreaming. But he felt substantial enough under her fingers. She traced the hard line of his jaw, her fingertips reading the muscles like Braille. At this late hour his skin felt whiskery, the bristles teasing her palm. She rubbed her hand against them like a nuzzling kitten.

Images of Ryan making love to her filled her mind, bewilderingly real, like forbidden fruit. Except that they were so close to becoming reality that dizziness gripped her.

She could feel his heartbeat, like a piston working deep in his chest, the rush of his lifeblood like a thunderstorm she could sense in her own body.

When had she become so attuned to him, as if they were one being instead of two? This was only supposed to happen between people who loved each other. It couldn't be happening to her.

But it was, and she parted her lips instinctively, excitement spiralling through her as he responded by deepening the kiss. She threaded her fingers through his hair, the strands feeling like silk.

The faint hint of a leathery aroma reached her. It was the aftershave lotion he'd been wearing when they set off on the bushwalk, hours ago. Traces of it remained, revived by the heat of his body. It was a tantalising discovery, like mapping a new country. She found she wanted to make more such discoveries, and set about exploring with her hands and mouth.

As she worried the buttons of his shirt, managing to unfasten the first few to reveal an expanse of deep, tanned chest, he caught her wrists and held her away from him. 'Stop, Terise.'

Rejection speared to the heart of her. There was a hard glitter in his eyes which made her go cold all over. Had he been playing with her? Horrified at how she had betrayed herself, she looked away, but he turned her face back to him. Tears glimmered in her eyes and he brushed at them with the back of his hand. 'What's this for?'

Awareness of what she had so nearly invited made her voice tremble. 'Isn't it obvious? You stopped because you don't trust me.'

'One has nothing to do with the other,' he said, his voice coldly precise. 'Unless you're planning a lifetime together, trust doesn't enter into it.'

And sometimes not even then, the thought seared through his mind. Commitment, even marriage didn't guarantee trust. He knew that well enough to write a book on it.

But this was Terise, not Clair, he told himself. They were worlds apart in character—as Terise had shown by risking her life to save Lisa. The knowledge should have overcome his reservations—Lord knew, his body was trying its hardest to convince him—but once bitten was enough. He hadn't got where he was by making the same mistake twice.

All the same, he was aware of an almost alien surge of regret as he heard the hurt vibrating in Terise's tone. 'Why, Ryan?'

He made himself sound cold and distant. 'Why did I start, or why did I stop?' For a crazy moment he was tempted to tell her everything, then he decided that the stakes were too high. Even if she swore she was protected, he couldn't take the risk. Not again.

'You can answer the first question by looking in a mirror,' he said instead. 'The answer to the second question is because I'm not about to risk another accident. I'm not prepared for this, and I doubt if you are either.'

She surprised him by shaking her head, confirming his assumption. His veneer of cynicism was threatened by the sudden conviction that she *hadn't* expected to find herself in his bed, so she hadn't taken precautions of any kind. Had he misread her after all?

He stood up, unwilling to reveal how shaken he was. 'I'll get you that painkiller now.'

It might help the pain in her ankle, she thought as he went into the bathroom. But what would he prescribe for the other pain, carving a tight band around her heart?

He came back with a capsule and a glass of water. 'The doctor said this should dull the pain and make you sleepy,' he said as he watched her take the tablet.

The medication worked quickly. As promised, the pain in her ankle dulled to non-existence and her thoughts became muzzy. It wasn't until she was almost asleep that she recalled what he had said. He hadn't made love to her because he didn't want *another* accident. What had he meant?

She tried to rouse herself sufficiently to ask him, but couldn't summon the strength. What did it matter anyway? She was nothing more than a challenge to him. What had he said? Trust didn't enter into it unless you were planning a lifetime together?

His plans for her were a lot briefer, she thought, hating the need which flared through her at the very idea. She knew that she'd have a hard time forgetting his embrace, and the heady demands of his kisses.

She shivered, contemplating what would have happened if he *had* been prepared. A stolen moment. An edge of danger. It had been all that and more. And, to her eternal shame, she knew that she would have gone right to the edge with him if he'd wanted her to.

It was a blessing when the medication finally pulled a velvet curtain over her whirling thoughts and she gave herself up to a restless sleep.

By the time they returned to Sydney Terise's ankle had healed and she was able to walk normally, with only the barest hint of discomfort if she overdid things.

Her inner pain refused to heal, and she was grateful that there were no outward signs—at least none that Ryan could read.

He still suspected her. She judged that by the close watch he had kept over her during her recovery and after they'd come home. He couldn't know it, but her feelings for him were his best insurance. Even if she could find any hint of scandal in his business or personal life—and she was beginning to doubt that she would—she wasn't sure that her courage would stretch to publicising it now.

It was a betrayal of herself and her stepsister, but it was the truth. She resolved to resign from Ryan's employ as soon as she could.

The thought of leaving Trudy and Lisa tore at her, but she pushed it aside. She would keep in touch with them somehow. Where there was a will, there had to be a way.

'Are you sure you're up to going shopping for the children's school clothes?' Ryan asked, breaking into her thoughts.

'I'll be fine,' she insisted. 'You've done enough, having your staff look after the twins while my ankle healed. It's time I pulled my weight.'

'Then I'll have Marcus accompany you,' he said in the tone of an order. 'I'd come myself, but we're on the downhill run with the bid. The host city is announced next week, and it will need every strategy we've got to keep Sydney as the front runner.'

'Marcus has enough to do without nursemaiding me,' she said, adding stiffly, 'Unless you don't trust me out of your sight.'

'Is there a reason why I shouldn't?' he asked, steel threading his rich baritone voice.

She felt a renewed fear that he did know who she was, and was playing her like a fish on a line. He probably thought that if he gave her enough rope she would hang herself. She forced a brittle laugh. 'Of course not. After our shopping, I plan to take the girls to see the Lego exhibition at Centrepoint, then to lunch as a treat. It's hardly cloak and dagger stuff.'

'Then there's no reason why Marcus shouldn't go along, is there?' he said, ending the discussion.

'No reason at all.'

Especially as she had no intentions of spending a whole day with the chauffeur as her watchdog, she thought mutinously. When she dismissed Marcus after he drove them to the shops he looked startled. 'The boss expects me to look after you.'

'If he objects, tell him I insisted,' she said. Two could play Ryan's game.

All the same, as Marcus drove away she felt a twinge of unease, recalling Clair's accusations against Ryan. He wouldn't hold Marcus responsible for her obstinacy, would he? She would hate the driver to suffer because of her. She reassured herself with the thought that Ryan might be tough, but she had only seen him act fairly so far. It was at odds with Clair's description of him, but not with Terise's own experience—confusing though it was.

Having the twins to herself assuaged some of her guilty feelings, and the shopping was soon done. They were queuing for tickets outside the Lego exhibition when a touch alerted Terise. 'What on earth are you doing here?'

She looked up into the curious hazel eyes of her stepmother. They'd spoken on the phone several times since Terise had begun working for Ryan, but her stepmother knew only the sketchiest details of her job. Luckily Elaine had been happy to chat about her own life, and hadn't seemed to notice any omission.

Now, however, she regarded the twins intently, a suspicious film of moisture blurring her gaze. 'These are the children you're looking after?'

Perhaps Terise was imagining things. Elaine was merely curious, that was all. 'Yes—this is Trudy and this is Lisa Westmore. We've been shopping for school clothes and I promised them a treat afterwards.'

'Hello, Trudy, Lisa. I'm Elaine, and I'm very pleased to meet you.'

Her eyes lifted to fix on Terise. This time there was no mistaking the emotion mirrored there. It caught at Terise's heartstrings as her stepmother said, 'I'd know them anywhere.'

'I don't know what you mean.' But she was afraid that she did.

'They're Clair's girls, aren't they?' Elaine said, in a voice barely above a whisper.

The queue moved forward and Terise bought tickets, aware that her stepmother had pushed a note forward for another adult ticket. How much had she guessed?

'Don't worry, I won't make a scene,' Elaine assured her as they filed into the exhibition. The children were immediately caught up in the magic of the life-sized models made out of thousands of tiny building blocks.

Terise touched Elaine's arm. 'I couldn't tell you. I wasn't sure how much you already knew.'

'I didn't realise who your charges were until I saw you together.' Her hand went to her mouth. 'They are so much like Clair at the same age that they couldn't be anyone else's children.'

'Then you knew about Clair's marriage?'

'I didn't find out until well after the event—and then by accident, when a friend showed me a newspaper cutting from the social pages. Evidently Clair told everyone she was an orphan.' Her eyes brimmed. 'Why would she do such a thing?'

'I don't know. She didn't tell me either, until much, much later.' She glanced at the children, but they were absorbed in the exhibition. 'I think she was pregnant when she married, and was too ashamed to tell us.'

Elaine nodded. 'It would explain a lot. I suppose once she started deceiving her husband she couldn't very well stop.'

Terise sighed. 'We'll probably never know the whole story.' Her breath caught in her throat as she realised Elaine might not know that her daughter was dead.

Her stepmother sensed her hesitation. 'It's all right, I know about the accident. After I found out she was married I made a point of checking the social pages afterwards, to see if anything was mentioned. It was a terrible way to learn such news.'

Elaine had been living in Sydney at the time of Clair's accident. Still, Terise wondered why her stepmother had chosen to suffer her tragic loss in silence. 'You should have let me share the burden,' she said.

Elaine's eyes brightened again. 'I hated to admit that my own daughter had cut me out of her life so completely. All I ever tried to do was love her and do my best for her.'

Terise squeezed her stepmother's hand. 'I'm sure she knew you did, in spite of everything.'

Elaine turned a wistful gaze towards Trudy and Lisa. 'And now I'm a grandmother. In a way, it's like having Clair back again. It lessens the hurt, somehow.' She gave a choked smile. 'Even if they don't know who I am, I'll always know it.'

'Of course you will. You're entitled to that much, at least.' It was little enough compensation.

Elaine clapped her hands. 'I know what we can do. I'll take the three of you to lunch. I've lent my flat to some overseas friends this week, so they can enjoy being near Manly and the beach, while I stay at the Menzies Hotel. We can go there.' She clutched Terise's arm. 'Please come. It would mean so much to me.'

Terise's mind shied away from all thoughts of what Ryan would say if he found out. She didn't want her fear to spoil Elaine's small pleasure, but she was sure that he wouldn't approve. She would consider the deception a part-repayment for his treatment of Clair. 'We'll come. I meant to take them to lunch, so the Menzies it is.'

Elaine's grateful look made Terise's heart turn over. Elaine had as much right to get to know the twins as Terise herself had—more, in fact, since they were Elaine's own flesh and blood. They were all the more precious to her for being the only legacy of her daughter.

Visiting Elaine's hotel pleased the twins—especially when she insisted on buying some of the Lego to take back with them. 'It will give them something to play with while we talk,' she said, when Terise demurred.

The Mandarin Suite was lavishly appointed, with a spacious living-dining-room, two bathrooms and beautiful Oriental décor.

Elaine noticed Terise's astonished look. 'I can't really afford this on my budget, but I need to splash out now and again to make myself feel better. I know what you're thinking—Clair got her expensive tastes from me—and you'd be right. I know I drove your father crazy, spending beyond our means, but it's just the way I am.'

Her apologetic shrug reminded Terise that Clair had always used her inability to change as her excuse too. Nothing she could say would help matters now, so Terise kept silent while Elaine ordered their lunch from room service. By the time it came the novelty of the hotel suite had worn off, and the twins were playing with their new Lego toys on the floor.

Terise gave them their lunch picnic-style on a tray, which they thought was great fun. It kept them from overhearing Elaine's murmured conversation.

'What is their father like? What sort of husband was he to Clair?'

'He's an excellent father,' Terise answered honestly. 'As for their marriage, you'd have to ask him.'

'But I can't. Clair saw to that.' She wrung her hands together. 'If I go to him and introduce myself I make Clair look bad, and I can't do it—I just can't.'

The alternative was to endure estrangement from her own grandchildren. Terise felt a surge of compassion for her stepmother, who would put her daughter's memory before her own needs. 'There's no easy solution, I'm afraid.'

Elaine dabbed at her eyes with a napkin. 'You're right. But, tell me, how did you get involved with Ryan Westmore? It must have been the most wonderful coincidence finding yourself in charge of his children.'

Terise debated whether to tell Elaine about Clair's letters, but decided against it. The woman had been through enough without having to face the possibility that her daughter's marriage had been desperately unhappy.

She explained about being mistaken for a temporary secretary at his Press conference, without explaining her reasons for going there in the first place. Elaine didn't push for details.

'It was meant to be,' she beamed. 'Now, tell me all about the children—their schools, their home-life, everything.'

Haltingly at first, then more fluently, Terise described life in the Westmore household, ending with a detailed description of the recent visit to the Bowral property.

By the time she had finished Elaine's face was drawn. 'You love him, don't you?' she said quietly.

Terise flicked a nervous glance towards the children, but their Lego tower absorbed their attention. 'Of course not,' she denied, feeling colour flood into her face.

Elaine reached for her hand. 'I've known you since you were a teenager, Terise. I lived through your first crushes and your first real love affair with that history teacher, and your sadness when it petered out. I know the symptoms, love.'

'But I can't be.'

The dismay in her voice made Elaine chuckle. 'Why not? We don't always get to choose whom we love. And it isn't a betrayal of Clair, you know.'

Ashamed, because that hadn't been the reason for her hesitancy, Terise looked away. 'I hardly know him.'

'I could have said the same of your father, but we made a good team, didn't we?'

'Yes.' The answer was truthful. Whatever Elaine's shortcomings, she had loved Terise's father and made him happy.

'Then what's holding you back? Marry the man. If nothing else, it will give me an excuse to visit my grandchildren.' There was more than a touch of irony in her tone.

Terise wondered how to tell her that she couldn't marry Ryan. Not only were his feelings clear on the subject, there was still the mystery of what sort of husband he had been to Clair.

Terise wasn't even sure she wanted to know any more. At least now she knew the reason for her cowardice, she thought ruefully. Elaine was right. She was in love with Ryan Westmore herself, and the thought of discovering anything bad about him filled her with apprehension.

'How could I have been so stupid?' she asked, half to herself.

'We're all a bit stupid when it comes to love. But it's even more stupid to let it slip through your fingers.'

'What if the man doesn't want your love?'

Elaine nodded sagely. 'So that's the problem. I thought there was more to this than you were telling me. Then, my dear, you have to *make* him want you.'

The idea of making Ryan do anything he didn't want to do brought a slight smile. 'Easier said than done,' she admitted.

Glancing at her watch, she jumped to her feet. 'Look at the time! I should have had the twins home an hour ago.' Caught up in talking to Elaine, she hadn't noticed the time passing. She could only hope that Ryan had decided to work late.

But luck was against her. By the time she had hailed a taxi outside the hotel and travelled the short distance home through peak-hour traffic almost another hour had gone by. Her heart was thundering as she escorted the twins into the apartment.

Ryan was waiting in the living-room, his expression ominous. 'Maggie has the children's dinner ready,' he observed, leaving volumes unspoken. 'Come and see me as soon as they're settled.'

How could she have been so stupid as to forget the time? she agonised as she handed the twins over to Maggie. It was tempting to remain in the cosy confines of the family-room, to avoid the storm awaiting her.

But Ryan was quite capable of dragging her out of here bodily, and she didn't want the children to witness a scene, so she squared her shoulders and returned to the living-room.

'I know we were late back, but——'

'Nearly two hours late,' he cut across her, anger scorching in his voice. 'Your explanation had better be good.'

CHAPTER EIGHT

Ryan's anger boiled away the last of Terise's enjoyment of the day. Granted, her late return put her in the wrong, but she didn't deserve the full force of his wrath. 'I do have an explanation, but I doubt you're in any mood to hear it,' she ventured.

His mouth twisted cynically. 'Try me.'

'I simply lost track of the time.'

Disbelief registered on his features. 'Like hell, you did. One of my assistants saw you going into the Menzies Hotel with the children.'

So he was spying on her now. Her backbone stiffened with annoyance. 'We went there for lunch. I told Marcus I'd take the children to lunch and I did.'

His eyes glittered a challenge. 'You weren't in any of the restaurants. I checked.'

Her sense of reality rocked in the face of his statement. 'You did what? This is outrageous. I know you don't trust me personally, but you acknowledge that I know my job. There's no justification for spying on me.'

His mouth thinned into a grim line. 'Strange as it may seem, I didn't intend to spy on you. When I was told where you were I had the misguided idea that it would be pleasant to join you for lunch. Can you imagine how I felt when you weren't in any of the public areas?'

It was the last thing she had expected. In the churning silence, she recognised a stab of pleasure at the thought of him abandoning his business commitments to make time for lunch with her and the children. If only she'd known.

There was nothing she could say except, 'I'm sorry. If I'd known you meant to join us, I'd have planned ahead. We were in one of the suites, having a room service lunch with a friend of mine.'

Instead of mollifying him, her comment added fuel to his anger. 'A male friend?'

When she caught his meaning her own anger rose. 'Of course not. How could you think such a thing? You know I put the children's welfare above everything. I love them. They're my family, for goodness' sake.'

In horror she realised what she'd said and rushed to make amends. 'I mean, they're like family to me.'

A mask dropped over his features, but it was somehow more chilling than his anger of a moment before. She flinched under the merciless scrutiny. 'I think you meant what you said the first time.' His hands flexed, as if he was imagining them around her throat. 'Am I finally close to getting the truth out of you?'

Her head swung from side to side in violent denial. 'No.'

'No, Terise? What are my children to you?' He moved closer, stalking her with the dangerous grace of a panther. 'You'd better tell me the rest or so help me I'll . . .'

Backed into a corner, literally as well as figuratively, she could only hurl words as weapons. 'You'll what? Treat me the way you treated my stepsister?'

As soon as the words had been said Terise would have given all she possessed to recall them. But it was too late. The light of battle already gleamed in Ryan's eyes.

He loomed over her, a study in controlled fury. 'Well, well. This is a night for revelations, isn't it? Don't stop now, my dear. Why don't we start with who you really are?'

He looked quite capable of shaking the information out of her. In fact, he looked as if he was barely restraining himself, so tightly were his fists clenched at his sides, his arms ramrod-straight. Only the knot of a muscle at his jaw betrayed the intensity of emotions he was holding in check.

This was how it would feel to be caged with a tiger, she thought, tremors gripping her slight frame. Faintness tugged at her consciousness but she fought it. Collapsing at his feet would be the coward's way out, and Terise O'Neill was no coward. Besides, it would only delay the inevitable confrontation.

Better to face him now, however daunting it was. She had a feeling that he would pursue her to the ends of the earth if that was what it took to get his answers. A man like Ryan didn't give up easily. Didn't give up at all, an inner voice insisted.

Well, neither did she. Wearily she lifted her head, injecting defiance into her gaze. 'You know who I am. I didn't lie about my identity.'

'You didn't lie about your professional background—as I established before entrusting you with the children. But there was a mystery about your personal life, and I dislike mysteries. Come with me.'

The turbulence in his expression was matched by the barely leashed violence in his movements as he took her arm. Half stumbling, she was towed to his study and thrust into a chair opposite his desk.

Shaken, she slumped in the chair, as disturbed by her chaotic thoughts as by his actions. Even now she still wanted him, she accepted unhappily. His anger—for which she couldn't in all conscience blame him—seemed to accentuate his maleness, to sharpen the qualities which made him so magnificent. He was like a raging bull, and she quailed at being the object of his rage, but part of her was fascinated and—yes—tantalised by it at the same time.

She could hardly believe the thoughts tumbling through her mind. How could she be thinking of him as anything but an enemy at this moment?

She knew only that enmity was the last thing she felt. A rising excitement wound through her, coiling her emotions ever tighter until she felt as if she would explode if she didn't find a safety valve soon.

There was none to be had in Ryan's expression. He looked as if he wanted to kill her.

He angled himself across the corner of his desk and picked up a red folder marked 'Confidential'. She waited tensely while he flicked through the contents. At last he drew out a sheet of paper and tossed the folder aside. 'Allow me to enlighten you.' His eyes flicked to the page and back to her.

'You were born in Bathurst, New South Wales. After your mother died of pneumonia, when you were seven, you and your father moved to Port Macquarie, where he had an elderly aunt. She died, leaving your father the house, where the two of you lived until his death.

'You didn't want to leave Bathurst, and this affected your performance at school. You became something of a rebel, then turned yourself around to become an exemplary student—largely due to the intervention of your teacher, Elaine Everson. She took up your cause and eventually married your father.'

He paused, consulting the folder again. His eyes bored into her as he continued, 'Elaine Everson, a widow, already had a daughter, didn't she?'

There was much more, but she barely heard it. Only a private investigator could have unearthed so much information about her family. Nausea came in waves at the thought of Ryan having her investigated as if she was some kind of criminal. She pressed her hands over her ears. 'How could you? I won't listen to any more of this. You have no right——'

The folder slammed on to the desk, the explosive sound making her jump. Alarm gripped her as he forced her hands down and held them at her sides. 'I have every right. Where my children are concerned nothing takes precedence, certainly not your delicate feelings.'

His fingers bit into her wrists. She made herself focus on the discomfort. It was better than giving free rein to the sensations which his touch unleashed in her. He was so close that his breath ruffled her hair. In the lamplight his eyes were silvery, hard, unyielding.

'Let me go,' she insisted, marvelling that she could sound so composed when a storm raged inside her.

He released her, and straightened without moving away. His fingers raked through his hair, leaving trails in the charcoal strands. For some reason the sight mesmerised Terise. It was an effort to look away. She massaged her wrists pointedly, although no damage had been done except to her pride. 'It seems Clair was right about you.'

Her comment rekindled Ryan's anger. 'Was she, now? About what?'

'About how you treated her.' A great aching chasm opened inside her as she said the words. How she had wanted them not to be true.

He moved then, stalking around the study like a caged predator. His circling movements brought him back to stand in front of her, his look accusing. 'Exactly how am I supposed to have treated her?'

She swallowed hard. 'Badly enough to make her drive away so recklessly that she was killed.'

'You were here, then? You saw what went on in our marriage?'

The bitterness in his voice stung her. 'Of course not. But when it all got too much she wrote and told me everything.'

His mirthless laugh sent goosebumps scudding along her spine. 'I'll bet she did. Did she also tell you she was supposed to be an orphan, with no family of her own?'

Long lashes feathered her cheeks as she looked away. 'I didn't know until you told me. She didn't have to pretend. She must have known we would have supported her.'

'You know she was pregnant when we married?'

'I guessed as much.'

'I'm not about to risk another accident.' His words echoed through her mind. Suddenly she understood his refusal to make love without the proper precautions.

Unwilling admiration overtook her. In spite of everything he had stood by Clair and cherished the children, although their conception must have come as a shock. 'It wouldn't have made any difference to me,' she assured him. 'Clair must have known that. Anyone can make a mistake.'

'But it wasn't a mistake,' he said, so quietly that she wondered if she was hearing correctly.

'You can't mean——'

'I mean exactly what I say. Clair's pregnancy was deliberate, to trap me into marrying her. She told me I had no need to take precautions because she was fully protected. I believed her—just as I believed her story about her background.'

Her mind whirled. What was he saying? 'I can't believe Clair would do something so underhand.' Yet she couldn't help recalling the times Clair had been flexible about the truth when they were teenagers.

'Naturally,' he said curtly. 'You're also prepared to accept her word that I mistreated her. What am I supposed to have done? Beaten her? Had affairs with other women? Neglected her? All of the above?' He loomed over her again. 'Come, now, I'm entitled to hear the charges against me.'

Terise stared dumbly at him. What did he expect from her? 'You said yourself I can't know what really happened,' she said, her voice hoarse.

His glittering gaze impaled her, refusing to let her off the hook. 'But you do know—or you think you do. I can see it in your face.' He spun aside, crashing his flattened palms against the desktop in a gesture of absolute frustration.

She winced, feeling the impact as if it radiated up her own arms.

'Well, I'm damned if I'll explain myself to you. You can think what you like and die wondering. It's no more than you deserve.'

His censure weighed heavily on her, although he was right—she did deserve it. He hadn't denied Clair's accusations, she noticed, and iced water trickled down her spine. More than anything she had wanted him to deny it outright. She bowed her head. 'I was wrong not to tell you about my relationship to Clair,' she admitted, 'but what I did tell you was the truth.'

A dismissive gesture greeted this attempt. 'Should I applaud your selective honesty? What did you hope to gain from your charade?'

His harshness lashed her. 'I don't know, and that is the truth.' She lifted misty eyes to him. She had come with the half-formed idea of making him pay for Clair's death. The last thing she had expected was to feel so confused, until she hardly knew her own mind any more.

If only she hadn't fallen in love with Ryan, things would have been simpler. She would have found something—anything—to use against him, and the score would have been settled. She hadn't counted on her own feelings getting in the way. Even now, in the face of his implacable anger, her desire for him was so strong that it rocked her to her core.

She bit her lip. It couldn't be love, this tumultuous blend of needs and desires he aroused in her. She had always envisaged love as a gentle, inexorable force, which would carry her away to some paradisical conclusion.

Never had she pictured it as a tidal wave, sweeping her off her feet and carrying her helplessly along, a heartbeat away from annihilation.

She shivered. 'What was I supposed to do? When she wrote to me, she sounded so depressed and lonely.'

'She always was a good actress.' With mechanical movements he went to a decanter set out on a tray and poured a generous measure of whisky into a glass. His hand wasn't quite steady, she noticed.

When he gestured to the decanter she shook her head. 'You have to see it from my side. She was my stepsister—the only sibling I'd ever had. She wasn't perfect, but I loved her.'

He downed most of the drink in a savage action. 'I don't have to do a damned thing. And stepsister is hardly a blood tie.'

Her shoulders lifted in a soul-weary gesture. 'I don't expect you to understand, but the relationship didn't matter. I'd always dreamed of having a sister.'

He barked a harsh laugh. 'And she took full advantage of it. I'll bet you spent your adolescence fighting her battles for her, taking the blame for everything, while she sat back and allowed it.'

The bitter truth of the statement was like a dash of cold water. She felt moved to defend herself, although he'd come uncomfortably close to the truth. 'I got a lot of benefits too, including a real family.'

'You're forgetting I was married to her. I suspect I knew her better than you did, because I don't look at the world through rose-coloured glasses.'

Her temper flared. 'And I do, I suppose?' She jumped to her feet, needing to pace off some of her frustration. 'Why are you doing this?'

'You need a dose of reality to jolt you out of this *Alice in Wonderland* world you live in.'

It was better than the cold reality he preferred. 'You're the person to administer this jolt, are you?' she demanded furiously.

'Somebody has to, for your own good.'

She gripped the back of the chair with fingers which were white to the bone. She suspected that her face was a similar colour. 'Your consideration for my welfare is touching but unnecessary, because I resign as of now. Is that what you wanted from me?'

She could hardly believe how much the simple statement hurt. The thought of walking away from him, and from the twins, chilled her blood. Would she even have the strength to do it? She must. He didn't love her. There was no place for her here.

'If I told you what I wanted from you, you'd run a mile,' he said. He gave a soft, humourless chuckle. 'Don't look so alarmed. Despite your stepsister's warnings, I do have some scruples. Unfortunately they don't extend to accepting your resignation.'

How could he expect her to stay? 'You can't stop me leaving,' she tried, wondering at the same time if there was anything he couldn't do.

Something unfathomable flickered in the icy depths of his eyes, as if he had read the unspoken fear in her. 'Can't I? Those two little girls in the other room might be a factor, don't you think?'

She could hardly believe it. He knew that she loved Trudy and Lisa, and yet he wasn't above trying to blackmail her into staying. 'You're despicable,' she spat out. 'How can you use your own children as bargaining chips?'

His shoulders lifted. 'My children aren't the bargaining chips. Your feelings for them are, and I'm hardly responsible for your feelings.'

'But you aren't above manipulating them to suit your own purposes.'

'See it how you will. The fact remains that I require your services until I can find a suitable replacement.'

So it was as simple as that. It wasn't that he wanted her to stay, only that he needed her to care for the twins until he found someone else.

The ache inside her increased until it was a physical pain, clutching like a tight fist around her heart. Everything he had said so far confirmed Clair's accusations. Terise should have been happy that she knew the truth at last. So why did she feel as if an abyss had opened at her feet?

A shiver shook her and she closed her eyes. According to their contract she had no choice but to stay until he released her. But she could put some emotional distance between them—would have to if she was to survive with some shred of pride intact.

He had said that he wasn't responsible for her feelings towards the children, shamelessly using them to bring her to heel. What would happen if he knew the full extent of her folly? If he knew that she loved him, what price might he not exact from her?

She started to turn stiffly away, a mask of professional detachment on her face. 'Very well, I'll stay until you can replace me.' She was quite proud to hear the statement made with only the faintest tremor.

'Until you can find enough evidence to hang me, don't you mean?'

The mask vanished, replaced by horror that he had read her intentions so accurately. He wasn't to know that she was no longer capable of doing anything to discredit him, no matter what she learned. It was a humiliating discovery. By falling in love with him she had gone over to the enemy, with no turning back. 'I wouldn't——' she began haltingly.

'But you meant to?' The question was a deadly caress of sound.

She closed her eyes. 'Yes.'

'I thought so. All fired up with righteous anger, you stormed in here intending to expose me for what I am.' It wasn't a question. None needed to be asked. He read the answer in her defeated body language. 'What will you do now, Terise?'

'I don't know.' It was the truth. She had never felt so confused before.

'Then I'll help you to make up your mind.'

With the lethal grace of a hunting tiger, he moved towards her. She stood her ground, mesmerised, until his arms around her waist snapped her back to reality. 'What are you doing?'

He pulled her hard against him, his hands wandering up and down her body as if she was a musical instrument that he could play with consummate skill. The moans which escaped from her throat did duty for the notes his questing fingers would have coaxed from such an instrument.

His mockery taunted her. 'You've decided I'm an ogre without conscience. I may as well live up to your expectations.'

Her pounding heart and laboured breathing were the products of her fury at his behaviour, not of his nearness, she told herself. Her eyes were level with his mouth, which was set into a determined line. She licked her lips and swallowed hard. 'You've already managed to do that successfully.'

'Then why haven't you run to the media with your story? It's the sort of sordid thing they'd love. I can't believe our confidentiality clause would be enough to stop you.'

'Because I——' She bit back the damning betrayal before she could say 'because I love you'. 'Because I'm not sure of my facts,' she substituted hoarsely.

'Perhaps you need more evidence.'

His arms tightened around her, and her nerves leapt as he claimed her mouth with ruthless thoroughness.

There was nothing gentle in the kiss. His mouth was hard and demanding, his teeth grinding against hers until her lips parted defensively. Then he plundered her soft palate with the skill of an expert, until her senses reeled and she clung to him, afraid that if she let go she would fall.

Shock made her keep her eyes open, and some part of her mind registered every plane and angle of his face and the dark, unreadable eyes devouring her. Then all conscious thought was eclipsed by sensation. Her pulse-beat raced and the blood surged through her veins like a thunderstorm. Never had she been so aware of her body as it pulsated in response to his demands.

Slowly she became aware of his reactions. It wasn't all on her side, she realised dazedly. He had meant to confirm her worst suspicions about him, but somewhere along the line things had changed.

The rapidity of his breathing, the thunder of his heart against her breasts and the unmistakable evidence of his arousal were almost overwhelming. She felt dazed, unable to believe that she could exert any sort of power over him.

When he half carried her towards the Chesterfield sofa, she had no will to resist. No matter what he was, or what he had done, she wanted him with every fibre of her being. Whatever his motives, she was his—and had been from the moment they'd met.

So she was unprepared when he pushed her roughly on to the sofa and spun away. 'Now do you have your evidence?'

He didn't mean to make love to her. She hunched her shoulders and linked her shaking hands around her knees, feeling utterly empty inside. The places he should have filled would remain aching voids for all time, she feared. He had never intended to love her, only to make her pay for her suspicions. 'A kiss proves nothing,' she snapped, channelling her disappointment into anger.

His back remained to her and the shoulder muscles tightened. 'You'd be surprised.' He whirled around, his eyes blazing. 'Yours proves that Clair stopped being the reason you stay here a long time ago.'

She managed to keep her gaze level, but was conscious of the burning patches on each cheek. How much had he discerned from her kiss? 'If you mean have I decided not to do you any harm, then, yes, I have. Does that satisfy you?' Desperately she hoped that it would. She wouldn't be able to bear it if he guessed the reason.

'Should I be grateful for your loyalty?' he ground out. 'If I'd known all I had to do was live up to your worst expectations, I'd have taken you to bed the day you arrived. It would have saved a lot of trouble.' He looked suddenly soul-weary. 'Go to bed, Terise. I'll start looking for your replacement as soon as I return from Canberra, after the result of the trade assembly bid is announced.'

She was shaking by the time she reached the sanctuary of her room. Thankfully Maggie had already bathed the twins and put them to bed, sparing her any more interactions tonight.

Ryan might have kissed her to pay her back for her accusations, but her responses were another matter. They warned her that living under his roof until he found a replacement was going to be an exquisite form of torture.

When the phone shrilled at her bedside, she jumped as if stung. Her emotions were too raw to deal with anything more tonight, but letting it ring might disturb the children. She picked it up, immediately recognising Elaine's voice.

She wanted to share her joy at finally meeting her grandchildren. 'We must do it again soon,' she enthused. 'They mean so much to me, Terise.'

There was no easy way to say it. 'I know, but it won't be possible. I resigned my job today.'

After a stunned silence, Elaine wailed, 'But that means I may never see Trudy and Lisa again.'

'I'm sorry, truly. But things aren't working out here.'

'Maybe I should speak to Ryan for you.'

'No, you mustn't.' The very idea filled her with alarm. It would be the final humiliation if Elaine told Ryan how she felt about him. 'Promise me you won't say anything?'

Tears threaded Elaine's voice. 'Very well. But it's too cruel—to find my grandchildren and lose them in the same day.'

It was how Terise herself felt, although by far the greatest heartache came from loving and losing the children's father. 'I know,' she said softly. 'I wish there was more I could do, but there isn't. I'm so sorry.'

'Sorry isn't an answer,' Elaine said, sounding injured. Then, a heartbeat later, 'But maybe there is an answer.'

'Elaine, what are you——?' But the phone buzzed with the sound of disconnection.

CHAPTER NINE

DURING the next few days Terise heard no more from Elaine. When she tried to contact her at the Menzies Hotel she was told that her stepmother had left. There was no answer when Terise rang the Queenscliff flat, which left her to wonder if Elaine had gone away somewhere.

Maybe it was for the best. The thought that she might decide to contact Ryan, in spite of her promise, disturbed Terise. Elaine was the only person who had suspected how Terise felt about Ryan. It was the last thing she wanted him to know.

Fortunately she saw very little of him. His time was almost wholly taken up with the final presentation for the world trade assembly bid in Canberra, in less than a week's time.

He still made time to spend with Trudy and Lisa, she noticed with a pang. Every night before they went to sleep he came into their room and read to them, or talked about their activities, giving no sign of the enormous pressure he was under.

At those times Terise made a point of having something else to do. These days she was too crushingly aware of her own feelings, like a siren song, tugging at her whenever he was around. He had said no more about finding a replacement for her, but she was sure he had the task in hand with his customary efficiency. He was so cold and distant towards her that she couldn't believe he wanted her around more than absolutely necessary.

She was surprised to be stopped by him as he emerged from the children's room one evening. The touch of his hand on her arm was so unexpected that she jerked away instinctively, her wounded look going to his face before she could stop herself.

He made a small sound of disgust. 'Must you react as if I was going to hurt you?'

How could he hurt her more than he already had? she thought bleakly. Her reaction had been a reflection of that inner hurt—one he didn't even know he had inflicted. Would never know if she could avoid it. 'You startled me,' she said.

His look was vexed. 'A jump, a cry—that's being startled. God, Terise, you don't have to be afraid of me, no matter what's been drummed into your head.'

It was easy to tell the truth. 'I'm not afraid of you.'

'Thank goodness for small mercies,' he said on an exasperated sigh. 'Do you think we can talk, or would you rather I rounded up Maggie to ride shotgun?'

'We can talk, if it's what you want.' He probably wanted to discuss her replacement. In spite of herself she felt a tight fist of pain clench around her heart. She had to leave. There was simply no choice any more. But it would be the hardest thing she had ever done.

She turned towards his study, but he indicated the living-room. 'You'll feel more comfortable in there, I expect.'

He didn't know it, but she could never feel comfortable around him again. Even the spacious living-room felt confining, and her breathing constricted as he sat down opposite the armchair she chose for herself. 'I suppose it's about my re-placement,' she began.

He looked blank, then his face tightened with disapproval. 'I haven't had time to do anything about that yet, so you'll have to endure another week here—at least until the host city is announced. I assume I can rely on you not to walk out before then?'

His lack of confidence made her wince. She looked down at the fingers twisting together in her lap. 'I've said I'll stay for now, and I will. You know I would never let Trudy and Lisa down.'

A deep V of annoyance etched his brow. 'Naturally you'd be concerned about the children. Your priorities are well known to me by now.'

They weren't, but she wasn't about to enlighten him. 'You wanted to discuss something with me?' she prompted. She wished he would get this over with. Being in the same room as him, her entire body aching with the need to be held by him, to feel his lips on hers, was almost more than she could bear.

The thought was sobering. If she found it this hard to endure when they were in the same room, how was she to survive a complete break? The thought brought a sob welling up from deep in her lungs, but she closed her mouth on the sound.

'The competing cities are to give final presentations to the trade assembly delegates in Canberra next week,' he went on, and she thanked her stars that he evidently hadn't noticed her near-breakdown. 'I'm flying down to present Sydney's final bid, then I'll stay until the announcement is made. There will be a lot of last-minute lobbying of the delegates, and we can't afford to let up until the decision is made.'

'It sounds exhausting,' she commented. She wished there was some way she could lighten his load, and realised that there was. 'If you're worried about the children, there's no need. I'll make sure they're well looked after.'

His grateful look almost broke her. 'I've explained to them that I have to go away. It isn't the first time, but it's the first since their mother...' He glanced away. 'They tell me they're big girls now, so I don't have to worry.'

In spite of her inner turmoil, Terise was forced to smile. 'I'll bet it was Lisa who said that.'

'Of course. The little mother. I've promised to telephone them every day, and they're excited about seeing me on television—since the bids will be televised around the world.'

'And I'll keep them so busy they won't have time to worry until you get back,' she assured him emphatically.

'I considered taking them with me, but it's not a good environment for children. Too much pressure and excitement.'

She nodded agreement, although she couldn't help wondering about his reasons for going alone. According to Maggie he was flying to Canberra with Cecily Elbrun. Terise had pretended uninterest, but her insides had clenched in protest. She told herself that she shouldn't have been surprised. He and Cecily were well matched, and she knew that he'd seen a lot of the Frenchwoman since they'd returned from Bowral.

With difficulty she kept her expression sanguine. 'They're better off in their own environment. They'll be at school a lot of the day, so you shouldn't worry too much.'

His smile deepened the shadows ringing his eyes. He was bone-weary, she saw with a shock. She had never seen anyone work so ferociously hard before. If Sydney didn't win the right to stage the world trade assembly, it wouldn't be from lack of commitment on Ryan's part.

They would win it, she thought fiercely, unwilling to entertain any other possibility. She wanted it for him, she acknowledged. If she couldn't have him for herself, she wanted to know that he was happy at least. The thought that it might be with Cecily Elbrun almost choked her, but she made herself face it. Hiding her head in the sand wouldn't change reality.

It hit her a moment later. This was real love, when the happiness of the beloved meant more than your own happiness. Giving—that was the secret. Giving with no thought of a return.

Unconditional love.

If only it wasn't so hard.

'And what about you?' he startled her by asking.

She made her tone light. 'What about me?'

'Have you thought what you'll do next?'

Die, came the immediate thought, but she rejected it as melodramatic. Nobody died of unrequited love. Suffered because of it, maybe—she knew that firsthand. 'I'll manage,' she said aloud, refusing to accept any other alternative. After all, what choice did she have?

His look hardened abruptly and his eyes became hooded. 'I dare say you will.' He stood up and stretched, bidding her a taut goodnight.

Next morning she walked into the living-room to find Cecily Elbrun already there. Dressed for travelling in a stylish silver-grey suit over a softly draping white silk blouse, she was leafing through the *Financial Review*. 'How is your ankle now?' she asked.

'Completely recovered, thank you.' Terise noted the Louis Vuitton luggage at Cecily's feet, and tried not to picture her and Ryan travelling together. 'I'm sorry my accident spoiled your visit to Bowral,' she went on. The apology had been on her mind ever since.

Cecily put her newspaper aside. 'I could hardly hold an accident against you. Ryan obviously had his hands full, so I took off. No harm done.' She smiled disarmingly and leaned forward. 'I understand you're leaving soon. Family reasons, according to Ryan.'

It was a tactful way of putting it. Terise nodded. 'I'll be going as soon as Mr Westmore arranges a replacement.'

A cool little smile greeted this statement. 'Ah, but a replacement may not be necessary.'

Terise looked blank. 'Why not?'

Cecily's Gallic shrug was accompanied by another smile. 'If Ryan is to—say—marry again, he won't need a nanny, will he?'

Misery descended over Terise like a cloak. Was Cecily telling her that she and Ryan were planning to marry? It wasn't unexpected, but she was surprised at how much the prospect hurt. She should offer Cecily her best wishes, but she balked at making the marriage seem more real than it did already. Now who was putting her head in the sand? She managed a wan smile. 'I hope everything goes well in Canberra.'

'It will.' Cecily was coolly confident. 'Ryan knows what he's doing.'

Terise allowed herself the luxury of nodding. 'All our prayers will be with him,' she said. In her case, he was taking much more: her heart, her dreams, her love, although he didn't know it.

The silence thickened between them until it was broken by Ryan's arrival. He carried a Gucci carry-on bag and a bulging leather briefcase. His notes for the presentation, Terise assumed, knowing that they wouldn't leave his sight until the job was done.

A thrill of pride to which she had not the slightest right rippled through her. He was dressed like any other businessman, in a superbly tailored dark suit which skimmed his athletic body, emphasising wide shoulders, trim hips and powerful legs. But there the similarities ended.

He would stand out in any crowd, she thought. Apart from an undeniable virility, he possessed that air of command, of leashed power, which was an aphrodisiac in itself.

Her hungry gaze lifted to his mouth, which was set in a taut line of determination. Small lines radiated around his mouth and eyes, testimony to the long hours he'd been putting in lately. But his eyes were bright with purpose, their intensity riveting as they came to rest on her.

Lord, how she loved him. The thought made her sway, dizzy with longings that she could not, would not name. No matter how foolish it was to feel this way, she knew that it would be a long time, possibly even a lifetime, before anything changed.

Her heart picked up speed as he moved closer. For an insane moment she fantasised that he would take her in his arms, his mouth telegraphing a farewell which would take her breath away. But all he said was, 'Can I leave everything to you now, Terise?'

Somehow she made herself answer. 'Yes. The children will be fine.'

'Good. I'll call every day.' He turned to Cecily. 'Ready, Madam Delegate?'

'Any time you are.'

'Then let's do it.'

The sound of their shared laughter stayed with Terise long after the door had closed behind them.

Ryan kept his promise to telephone every day, although it wasn't always at the same time, depending on his hectic schedule. But they always knew where he was and what he was doing, because the assembly's deliberations were televised for the news each evening. The twins could hardly contain their excitement at seeing their father on television, but for Terise every interview was slow torture.

She would have talked herself out of watching the actual announcement if Maggie and Marcus hadn't decided to watch it with her. It was late, and the twins were already in bed by the time they settled down by the television set.

The camera was tracking new arrivals up a red carpet leading to the banquet-room. A tight knot of pain squeezed Terise's heart when she saw Ryan arrive with Cecily on his arm.

'Don't they look glamorous?' Maggie said excitedly.

A journalist thrust a microphone in front of Ryan and Cecily. 'I hear there could be another announcement made tonight—a wedding announcement. Would you care to comment?'

Terise's heart skipped a beat as Ryan shook his head. 'Only one announcement concerns us tonight—the host city for the next world trade assembly.'

Terise felt her knees buckle and stumbled to a chair, her vision blurring. Hunching her knees up under her chin, she tried to listen to the announcer, but all she kept hearing was 'a wedding announcement...a wedding announcement'. Ryan and Cecily? It had to be. The only reason Ryan didn't want it announced immediately was to avoid overshadowing the news of the bid.

She didn't care, she tried to tell herself. Ryan was nothing to her—an accident of chemistry, no more. He and Cecily were well matched. So why did she feel as if her world had spun to an end?

Her throat aching, she started to leave the room, but Maggie caught her arm. 'You can't go now; they're about to make the announcement.'

The only one which meant anything to her had already been made, but she sat down with robotlike obedience. Despite the pain clenching her heart, she couldn't wish anything for Ryan but a successful outcome.

She held her breath as the president of the world trade council got to his feet and read from a prepared speech in heavily accented tones. His words—some kind of testimony to the bidding cities—were a blur of sound to Terise. She was so caught up in her own misery that she almost missed his final words. 'The next world trade assembly will convene in Sydney, Australia.'

Then Maggie and Marcus caught her up in a mad embrace. Maggie dabbed her eyes. 'I knew he'd do it, God bless him.'

Terise's own cheeks were wet as she accepted a glass of champagne from Marcus. 'Here's to Ryan and his team.'

She tried to shut her eyes to the sight of Cecily flinging herself into Ryan's arms—a sight which the cameras replayed over and over during the next few minutes. It was a sight she might as well get used to, she supposed, knowing in her heart that she never would.

Marcus and Maggie had retired to their own quarters and Terise was clearing away the signs of celebration when the telephone rang, sounding loud in the night stillness. She picked it up, going cold all over when she heard Ryan's voice. 'We saw the announcement on television. Congratulations,' she said in a choked voice.

He sounded infinitely weary. 'We did it on one vote—can you believe it?'

Cecily's vote, she assumed. It was the least the woman could have done for the man she was to marry. 'Congratulations on both counts,' she said, in a voice which shook so hard that it was a wonder she made sense. 'For the successful bid and the announcement about Cecily.' There, she'd managed it without disgracing herself. Luckily he couldn't see the tears coursing silently down her cheeks.

'How did you hear about that?' He sounded wary. 'It wasn't supposed to get out until after the banquet. I'm due there as soon as I get past the media gauntlet waiting for me.'

'Enjoy yourself,' she said mechanically, torn between wanting to keep him on the phone and needing him to hang up before she broke down completely.

He laughed. 'I'll be lucky if I can stay awake. Tell the kids I'm flying home tomorrow afternoon, after I see the Prime Minister. Damn, it will be good to get home.'

But not to her, she thought, breaking her own vow to be strong. 'I'll tell the children. They'll be thrilled.'

'And you? Are you thrilled, Terise?'

For him, yes. For herself, she was heartsick. It was only a matter of time before his engagement to Cecily became public knowledge—possibly even tonight. Then this part of her life would be over. The best part, she couldn't help thinking.

'I'm very happy for you,' she managed, although she had never felt so desperately unhappy.

For the first time since her teens, she cried herself to sleep that night.

By the next afternoon she had recovered her composure sufficiently to greet him almost normally when he walked in from his flight. The sight of his bone-weary expression was almost her undoing. She had never seen him look so drained. 'Can I get you a drink?' she asked.

He brightened, but she could see that it took an effort. 'It's tempting, but it would probably finish me off. Being back and having you waiting is tonic enough for now.'

Her heart turned over. Meaningless platitudes, she told herself. Don't read anything into it. 'Did Cecily fly back with you?' she forced herself to ask.

He shook his head. 'She's heading for Germany with the president of the assembly, and won't be back for two months.'

Was this the reason for his drained look? 'Why don't you have a bath and a rest while I pick up Trudy and Lisa?' she suggested with brisk professionalism.

'I haven't put my car away yet. I'll drive you to the school.'

The prospect of his company made her short of breath. 'There's no need, when you're obviously all-in.'

He frowned. 'Distasteful as you apparently find my company, you'll have to grin and bear it, because I want to see my children. Just give me a minute to change.'

He disappeared into the bedroom, emerging a short time later in a teal polo shirt and jeans. He had shed some of his weariness with his business attire, but made no protest when she offered to drive.

When they stopped at the traffic lights she glanced at him. His head was tipped back and his eyes were closed. She studied his profile greedily, an ache starting up inside her. She fought it down. She wasn't about to take advantage either of his exhaustion or of Cecily's absence to take what didn't belong to her.

When did you get to be such a saint? she asked her reflection in the driving-mirror.

Not a saint, a realist, she told the reflection. She could never be satisfied with the crumbs of a relationship with him. It was all or nothing, and since she couldn't have it all . . .

'We're here,' she told Ryan gently as she pulled up outside the school.

Trudy and Lisa were nowhere in sight. Their teacher looked surprised to see them. 'Their grandmother collected them on your instructions,' she said. 'They left ages ago.'

Ryan looked as if he would explode. 'Their *what*?'

Terise clutched his arm, feeling faint. 'Oh, Elaine, how could you?'

He shook off her arm, spinning her to face him. 'Do you know something about this?'

Tension coiled through her as she felt the colour leave her face. She nodded, and managed to explain about Elaine wanting to see the children.

He gave her a slight shake. 'How did she know where to find them? She's had no contact with me.'

'It's my fault,' she confessed. 'Elaine was the friend I saw at the Menzies. She wanted to know everything about the children.'

His eyes blazed. 'And you didn't think it worth mentioning to me?'

The teacher stopped wringing her hands long enough to contribute. 'She had plenty of identification, and she knew the children well. They were so pleased to see her, otherwise I'd never have allowed them to go with her.'

He refused to be mollified. 'Your security will need urgent review before I allow my children to return.'

'Of course, Mr Westmore.'

Terise retrieved his attention. 'Please don't blame the school, Ryan. It's all my fault.'

He jerked her towards the car. 'Then start making amends. Get into the car.'

She offered no resistance as he dragged her to the vehicle and thrust his mobile phone into her hands. 'Call this woman. I want to speak to her now.'

With shaking hands, Terise dialled Elaine's number, and almost wept when she answered right away. Ryan took the phone from her and subjected Elaine to a cold, merciless quiz until he was satisfied that the girls were in no danger. Then he slammed the phone down, an explosive outpouring of breath whistling between his clenched teeth.

Frightened, Terise took in the rigid lines in his face and the set of his back. His hands gripped the steering-wheel so tightly that she expected it to snap. 'Trudy and Lisa are fine,' she said gently, in case the fact hadn't yet registered. 'Elaine loves them. She wouldn't hurt them.'

The look he shot her was furiously accusing. 'You still don't get it, do you? The last member of my family to be snatched from my life I didn't see again for five years.'

The car reeled around her as she saw the connection. 'Oh, God, Ryan. I'm so sorry. I didn't realise.' In the last few minutes he had relived the horror of his father's kidnapping. She also now understood why he had been so angry when she was late bringing the twins home. 'Elaine didn't know how you'd see her actions,' she whispered, holding her hands out to him in mute appeal.

'She will when I'm finished with her,' he vowed.

She let her hands drop, his rejection palpable. 'Please don't be too hard on her,' she begged. 'You lost a wife, but Elaine also lost a daughter. Trudy and Lisa are the only blood relatives she has left.'

'I might have known you'd side with her. Self-ishness obviously runs in your family.'

He drove fast but with icy precision, following her stilted directions to Elaine's flat in Queenscliff. She could think of nothing to say to alleviate his pain—or her own distress.

Loving is giving, she reminded herself. He needed her strength right now, no matter what it cost her.

He was very near the edge of his endurance. The thought strengthened her. If all she could do was be there for him, as a safety valve if necessary, then that was what she would do.

Elaine was white to the eyes when she opened the door to them. Ryan said nothing to her until he'd checked on the children, who were playing happily with the Lego set in the living-room. Then he dragged the older woman into a bedroom, out of earshot. 'What the hell do you think you're playing at—kidnapping my children?'

Elaine shuddered. 'I meant to bring them home soon. I only wanted to spend a little time with them.'

Her plea was lost on Ryan. 'The only reason I didn't arrive with the police was to avoid upsetting Trudy and Lisa. But if this *ever* happens again, I swear I'll bring formal charges.'

Elaine looked faint, and Terise automatically interposed herself between her stepmother and Ryan. 'That's enough. Can't you see she's on the point of collapse?'

Elaine mewed a protest. 'He's right, Terise. It was the wrong thing to do, but I was desperate.' She glanced through the doorway to the children. 'They mean so much to me. I meant to bring them home before you returned from your trip.'

'Which your stepdaughter helpfully told you about,' he assumed, his baritone voice vibrant with anger.

Horror filled Terise's gaze. 'You can't think I was a party to this?'

Ryan gripped her arms, his fingers biting cruelly. 'You'd better not have been.' He dropped her arms abruptly, apparently aware of how tenuous his control was. 'I'll take my children now.'

Her head spun as she rounded up Trudy and Lisa, doing her best to reassure them. Elaine's white face and her silence frightened them, as did the aura of tension Ryan projected, but his voice was gentle as he ushered them out of the flat.

When Terise moved to follow he shook his head. 'Stay with your stepmother. We'll be fine without you.'

'We'll be fine without you'. The words reverberated through her mind, cruelly final. He didn't want to have any more to do with her. She could hardly blame him after what had happened, but it felt as if a part of her had been torn out by the roots.

Her last sight was of his cold, set face, his features etched with a weariness which tore at her heart. Oblivious to his state of mind, the twins clung to his hands, chattering excitedly about their adventures with Elaine.

Closing the door between them, Terise gave a sigh of despair. She turned to her stepmother, who was wringing her hands in the background. 'Oh, Elaine, what have you done?'

CHAPTER TEN

ELAINE pulled herself together with an effort. 'What can I say? After all my years as a teacher I did the unpardonable—taking children away from school without their father's permission.'

'You meant well.' The excuse was as lame as it sounded.

'And we both know what road is paved with good intentions.' She shuddered visibly. 'I'll probably never see them again, and it's all my own fault.'

Terise put her arms around her stepmother. When had she become so slight, so fragile, as if her bones would crack under pressure? 'Don't upset yourself any more, please. It isn't going to help.'

Elaine's wide eyes searched her face. 'How can you be so forgiving, when I've ruined things between you and the man you love?'

Shock jolted through Terise at hearing the terrible reality put into words. 'You didn't,' she denied, without much conviction. 'He doesn't love me, so there was nothing to ruin. After he found out I was Clair's stepsister, it was all over anyway.'

'He tarred you with the same brush?'

When Terise would have denied it, Elaine took her hand and led her back to the living-room, urging her to sit down. 'Don't look so shocked. I know how he felt about my daughter. No wonder, if things were as bad as I think they were.'

She held up a hand as Terise tried to demur. 'It's all right. I loved my daughter, but I'm not blind. I know she pulled the wool over your eyes when you were younger. I didn't say anything because I wanted so much for us all to get along—to be a family. Perhaps it wasn't entirely fair to you, but I took her side because you were so much stronger. I felt you could cope better.'

The unfairness of it stung Terise, but it was all in the past now. Nothing would be served by saying what was in her mind—that she hadn't been strong at all, and had bitterly resented the way Elaine had sided with her own daughter. It had made Terise feel less valued. 'We can't change what's past,' she observed.

Elaine sighed. 'You're right. All the same, I made a complete mess of things today, didn't I? But I wanted to see my grandchildren again. With you about to leave Ryan's employ, I couldn't think of anything else.'

Terise hugged her arms around herself, feeling suddenly cold although the afternoon was warm. 'Oh, Elaine, this whole situation is a complete mess. Sometimes I wish...'

'That Clair had never involved you in her affairs?' Elaine completed the thought.

Terise regarded her stepmother in surprise. 'You knew her marriage was in difficulties?'

'I knew she was *causing* difficulties. She called me just once, trying to convince me that Ryan was a bad husband to her. She wanted to run away and bring the children to me, to get even with him. Much as I wanted to meet them, I couldn't encourage her. I advised her to seek professional counselling. She owed her children that much at least.'

Terise inclined her head, wishing she'd thought to offer similar advice. 'It was sound advice, but she didn't take it. She wrote to me instead.' The admission was like ashes in her mouth. 'I received two letters all about how cruel Ryan was.'

Compassion softened the lines of Elaine's face. 'So you came to the city to see for yourself. It was a pity you were caught up in Clair's problems. She was always dragging you into some scheme or other, wasn't she?'

'I didn't mind. She was my sister, and I thought sisters supported each other. But this time she was playing with people's lives.' Terise sighed softly. 'At first I didn't know what to think, but I've come to know Ryan. He has a fierce temper but he's always just.'

'As I saw for myself today.' Elaine twisted her wedding-ring round and round on her finger. Terise was mildly surprised that she still wore it. 'He could easily have handed me over to the police.'

The idea shook Terise anew. 'It's a miracle that he didn't, given his own history.'

'How do you mean?'

Haltingly Terise told Elaine about Ryan's father being kidnapped and held hostage. 'It was five years before he saw his father again,' she concluded.

An agony of shame gripped Elaine, her distress mirrored in the troubled eyes she turned to Terise. 'And I brought back the memories. No wonder he reacted so badly.'

'But you weren't to know.'

A glimpse of the skilled teacher Elaine had been surfaced briefly. 'Ignorance is no excuse. I'll make sure he understands that it will never happen again—even if it means I never see Trudy and Lisa. He's a good man and a good father. He deserves better than to wonder if I'm waiting for the chance to snatch them again.'

Pride in her stepmother swelled within Terise, although she could see what the decision had cost her. 'He can't ask more of you than that.'

'As you say, he's a fair man.' Elaine took a deep breath and stood up. 'You'd better stay the night here. The spare bedroom is made up, so you'll be comfortable there.'

She wouldn't be comfortable anywhere away from Ryan, Terise knew. But he had made it clear that he didn't want her around. After today she could hardly blame him. She knew precisely how her stepmother felt. Her grandchildren were now off-limits to her—just as Ryan was to Terise. But knowing that she could never see him again and living with the fact were two different things.

*   *   *

'Shall I get you something else?' Elaine asked her gently, when Terise barely picked at the meal she prepared.

Elaine's plate was also untouched. Terise shook her head. 'No, I'm not hungry.'

'Then I'll put the kettle on. I don't know what it is about a cup of tea, but it's the universal panacea.'

It was worth a try, so Terise nodded. Elaine removed the plates of food and disappeared into the kitchen, leaving Terise alone with her tangled thoughts.

But she was denied even that respite, when the telephone shrieked a summons. She jumped, her nerves badly on edge. Could it be Ryan? She immediately chided herself for her foolishness. It was more likely to be one of Elaine's friends on a social call.

'Could you answer it?' Elaine called from the kitchen.

With an unaccustomed feeling of foreboding, Terise picked up the phone. 'Is a Ms Terise O'Neill there?' came the surprising query.

'Yes, I'm Terise O'Neill.' Who besides Ryan knew where she was or had this number?

'I'm sorry to disturb you. I'm calling from the Royal North Shore Hospital. A relative of yours has been admitted, and you were the only person we've been able to contact.'

The only relative she had was in the kitchen making tea. Terise cleared her throat. 'There must be a mistake.'

'I don't think so. You are Mr Ryan Westmore's sister-in-law?'

She went cold from head to foot. 'Yes, I am.'

'There's no easy way to tell you this, but he was in a car accident on the Sydney Harbour Bridge. There was no answer at his home number, and then someone had the presence of mind to press the redial button on his mobile phone, and we got this number. Mr Westmore was conscious for a few minutes, long enough to tell us your name and your relationship to him.'

Conscious for a few minutes... Terise felt the room spin around her and clutched the back of a chair. 'Please, he isn't...?'

'He's alive, and not badly injured. He's being treated for concussion and severe bruising.'

She could hardly bring herself to ask, 'The two little girls who were with him?'

'They were luckier. Thank goodness Mr Westmore had the sense to put his children in the back seat, securely fastened into child restraints. I wish more parents——'

'Please, are they all right?' Terise couldn't wait for the woman to finish her homily.

'I'm sorry. Yes, they are. We're keeping them in the children's ward overnight for observation, but they suffered no injuries.'

Terise released a strangled breath. 'Thank God. Can I see Ryan and the girls?'

'It would help if you came, although he isn't conscious as yet. We need someone to reassure the children and take care of the paperwork.'

'I'll be there in fifteen minutes.' Hanging up, Terise shook from head to foot. She should never have allowed Ryan to drive in his exhausted condition. Never mind that no power on earth could have stopped him. It made her feel less guilty to punish herself with such thoughts.

Elaine swiftly dealt with such notions. 'There was nothing you could have done,' she said severely. 'It's the worst kind of arrogance to think you can solve all the world's problems.'

She sounded so much like the teacher Terise had first known that she managed a wan smile. 'You're right. Once Ryan makes up his mind, it's like trying to turn a raging bull.'

Elaine all but pushed her out of the door into a taxi. 'Well, this raging bull is going to need your strength tonight. Go to him and tell him you love him.'

Terise turned a white face to her. 'I can't . . .'

'Think how close you came to losing him tonight before you tell me that.'

Her words haunted Terise all the way to the hospital. She went through the motions of completing forms on Ryan's behalf, barely aware of what she was signing. At last they let her see the twins, who were curled up in chairs watching a children's video.

'We had ice-cream for tea,' they told Terise importantly.

They accepted their confinement with the equanimity of six-year-olds, only becoming anxious when they asked about their father. Terise reassured them as best she could, desperately wishing that someone could reassure her.

Her nerves were at screaming point when she was finally admitted to the private room where Ryan lay.

Her heart turned over at the sight of his powerful figure lying still as death under the light covering. Tubes ran from his arm to a unit beside the bed. Above him, a screen silently monitored his vital signs. His eyes were closed.

Her insides quivered as she approached the bed, stretching out a tentative hand to stroke the side of his dear, bruised face. A bandage masked an injury to his forehead, doubtless the cause of the concussion.

'Oh, Ryan, I do love you,' she said, on a tortured outpouring of breath.

A groan slid from him and he stirred restively, straining against the restriction of the tubes and monitors. He couldn't stand being restrained, even in unconsciousness, she thought with a faint smile.

It vanished as his eyes began to open. She took his hand, her grip tightening so that he would know he wasn't alone. 'Ryan, can you hear me?'

'God, my head. Must have been some party.'

His words were slightly slurred, making her wonder if she had heard correctly. She leaned into his line of vision. 'Do you know where you are?'

His eyes opened fully, but there was a strange quality in them as he looked at her, wrestling with his thoughts. 'What're you doing here, Clair?'

He didn't know who she was, she realised with a sickening jolt. He thought she was his late wife.

'I had to come. I care about you,' she tried again.

He gave a bitter laugh. 'That's rich, Clair. First time you've come to... my room since... children born.'

'Why, Ryan?' she asked, feeling hideously uncomfortable. He obviously didn't know what he was saying, but she had to know.

'No need,' he murmured. 'You got... what you wanted,' he ground out, through a thick haze of pain and confusion. 'You're my wife now... Got it all without... no need for... wifely obligations.'

She couldn't let him go on. 'Ryan, don't, please. I can't bear to see you like this.'

He rolled his head from side to side, his teeth grinding loudly enough for her to hear. She reached for the call button to summon the nurse. He was obviously in pain.

But a strong hand snapped out and fastened around her wrist. 'Cut out the act, Clair. You don't care about me. You don't even care about your own children.' He sounded almost lucid but his eyes were fever-bright.

'Your fancy new car...I paid for...is a two-seater. No family outings for you.' A groan found its way up from deep in his chest. 'Go to your party, then. I won't stop you. Roads wet...take care...'

The tears rolled down Terise's face unchecked, splashing on to his hand clamped around her wrist. He must be reliving the night Clair had been killed, apparently going to a party he'd tried to talk her out of attending because the roads were bad.

'Ryan, stop. I'm not Clair. She died in that car, driving too fast. Try to remember.'

Relief coursed through her as she saw his eyes regain focus. His brow creased with the effort of recalling where he was and how he had got there. 'Terise? I thought you were... Where am I?'

'You were in a car accident. You're in hospital,' she told him.

Alarm streaked across his face and he half rose from the bed. 'Trudy and Lisa?'

Her hands gripped his shoulders, easing him back against the pillows. He was burning with fever. 'It's all right, they're fine. Not a scratch.'

'Thank God.' He closed his eyes. She waited a few minutes, to see if he would open them again, but his breathing settled to a reassuring evenness.

She caressed his brow, smoothing away some of the worry lines as she crooned meaningless words under her breath. When she was sure he was asleep, she pressed her lips to his forehead. 'I love you, Ryan. More than life itself. Get well for me, please.'

She dragged an armchair closer to the bed and sat down, linking her fingers with his. In this position, she could keep watch without disturbing him. Her thoughts spun with the things he had inadvertently revealed.

She'd already known that Clair had trapped him into marriage through her pregnancy—a fact she had been too ashamed to share with her family. So she had told him that she was an orphan. Then, it seemed, she had made the most of her position as his wife without accepting any of her obligations.

How must Ryan feel, knowing that his money had bought the fast car in which his wife had died? No matter that he wasn't to blame. He must have paid for her sins many times over in self-recrimination. Terise knew only too well how that felt, having been made a scapegoat for Clair too often herself.

Hardest to forgive must have been Clair's attitude towards the twins. How could any mother have used her own children so shamelessly? Especially such adorable little girls as Trudy and Lisa. They were already so deeply anchored in Terise's heart that she couldn't bear the thought of anyone failing to cherish them.

How could she have been such a fool as to believe Clair's lies? The fault had all been on her side—not on Ryan's. Bored with marriage, she had invented her tales of mistreatment to bring Terise running. To Terise's shame, it had worked. She had come charging in like an avenging angel, looking for ways to hurt a man who had already been hurt more than anyone deserved to endure.

Thank goodness she hadn't succeeded, she thought as tears rolled unheeded down her cheeks. She swabbed them away angrily. Self-pity was a luxury now. Her concern must be for Ryan. She couldn't undo the harm already done, but she could avoid inflicting more pain on a man who had shouldered enough to last a lifetime.

If it meant leaving him she would do it, she told herself decisively. Never mind what it would cost her. She would count that later. For now, all she wanted was his happiness.

Unconditional love, she thought again. Giving more than you received. It was his right.

She was unaware of drifting off to sleep until she was disturbed by a nurse fussing with the intravenous lines. 'Sorry to disturb you,' she mouthed as she completed her work, adding a notation to the chart at the foot of Ryan's bed.

Terise's neck ached, and her mouth felt as if it was stuffed with cotton wool. According to her watch she'd been here for hours. 'How is he?' she queried softly.

The nurse checked the monitors. 'Sleeping normally. He should be well enough to go home soon.'

Joy surged through Terise, and her eyes blurred until she blinked them clear. This was no time for tears. He was going to be all right.

With a reassuring smile the nurse left them, and Terise stretched to ease her cramped muscles. Ryan still gripped her hand, limiting her movements, but she welcomed the tightness in her joints. It was little enough sacrifice for all he'd been through.

Suddenly she sensed his eyes on her, open and aware now. His hand tightened on hers, refusing to let her withdraw. 'How long have you been here?'

'Most of the night.'

'Did I hear you say the children are all right? I wasn't dreaming?'

She lowered her head. 'No, you weren't dreaming. They escaped without a scratch. You got the concussion.'

He raised a hand to his head. 'That explains the king-sized headache. The other driver was drunk, weaving all over the bridge. I was too tired, my reflexes too slow to get out of his way.'

'The police arrested him. Don't think about it now,' she urged, having heard the details from the admissions staff. 'Save your strength for your recovery.'

He really looked at her then, his eyes narrowing in the lowered light. 'You *are* here. You know, I had the damnedest dream...'

She looked away. 'It wasn't a dream. You mistook me for Clair and told me a few home truths.'

He frowned. 'You can't believe everything a man with concussion tells you.'

'Even if it's what I want to believe?'

He made a noise of disapproval, but she ignored it.

'It's all making sense now. It must have been hell for you. Why didn't you tell me when I made all those stupid accusations?'

'It wouldn't have changed what happened.'

She looked at him in wonder. 'And you wanted to protect her memory for the children's sake.' It explained his anger when he had found her gossiping about his marriage with Maggie.

'You and your rose-coloured glasses,' he growled. 'But this time you're right. Ours was no more than a marriage of convenience. If it hadn't been for Trudy and Lisa...' His hand clenched in hers. 'Clair enjoyed the status more than the reality of being a wife. I lived with it for my kids. They made everything worthwhile.' He started to sit up, swearing as the room swam around him.

She slid an arm around his shoulders. 'Why don't you lie still and be glad you're still alive?'

'Because I can think of much better things to do.'

Before she could react he had wrapped her in his arms and pulled her down on to the bed with him.

It felt so wonderful that she was almost tempted to allow it, until she recalled her promise to herself. 'Let me go, Ryan. This isn't the answer.'

'It is if you meant it when you said you love me.'

Colour rioted across her features. 'I thought you were asleep.'

'Did you mean it, Terise?'

There was nothing else to say. 'Yes.'

'And I love you. It's all that really matters.'

It was all happening too fast. She had never dreamed that Ryan returned her love. It was almost too much to take in. 'But you can't. What about Cecily?'

His lips sought her neck and explored it as he said in a muffled voice, 'I told you, she's on her way to Germany with her fiancé—the president of the world trade assembly.'

Her heart did a somersault. 'You left out the most important word. Fiancé,' she said huskily. '*That* was the wedding announcement the media were expecting? But I thought you and Cecily...'

He had started on her ears now, and heat tore through her like wildfire. 'Cecily is an old and dear friend—no more. I told her how I felt about you at Bowral, which is why she left us alone.' He finally reached her mouth. 'It worked, didn't it?'

'It almost didn't,' she said, freeing her lips with a curious reluctance. 'When you found out how I'd deceived you I thought it was the end of everything.'

He sobered abruptly. 'It could have been. I'd begun to fall in love with you after you risked your neck to save Lisa on the mountain. Seeing you injured almost killed me, so it had to be love.'

'Then you found out the truth.'

'It tore me apart. I thought you were like Clair, and I wasn't about to go through that again. But everything about you was so different. When they carried me in here all I thought about was maybe never having the chance to tell you I love you.'

She had never thought to hear him say it, and the possibility that he might have died without ever saying it frightened her so badly that she began to tremble.

He understood and held her tightly, soothing her with murmured endearments as he stroked her hair and peppered her face with kisses.

Half lying on the hospital bed, she surrendered to the ecstasy of his arms around her and the passion she read in his kisses, until she was dizzy with wanting him.

Suddenly he looked up and laughed, tracing the side of her face with a teasing finger. 'You realise half the hospital knows what you do to me by now?'

Following his gaze to the heart monitor above the bed, she saw a frantic tracing of peaks and valleys as big as the Himalayas—a visible reminder of how she stirred his blood. She hid her head against his shoulder, her face flaming.

He lifted her chin, his eyes caressing. 'Never be ashamed of our love, my darling. I don't care if the whole world knows it. We've waited long enough for our happiness.'

Waiting a little longer was the sweetest torment, she found, trying to weigh it against a lifetime of happiness ahead. There was so much to do before their wedding—even after Ryan had finished recuperating.

The ceremony was held in the grounds of Westmoreland at Bowral, on a day God had decreed should be perfect for a wedding.

Trudy and Lisa looked adorable, in identical gowns of coral silk, with garlands of flowers on their blonde heads. Each carried a basket of rose petals to strew before the bride.

Along this scented path Terise walked, in a haze of pure happiness, her crushed silk gown whispering around her legs. Admiration was reflected in the looks turned to her from Maggie, Marcus and Elaine, and Ryan's many friends. He had flown his mother, Patricia, out from England a few days before, and she bestowed a smile of encouragement as Terise passed her. Cecily Elbrun—or Cecily Kurtz, as she was now—looked smugly satisfied on the arm of her new husband.

But Terise had eyes only for the man waiting for her in front of the celebrant. Ryan's injury had bequeathed him a dashing scar over one eye and a slightly leaner profile. He looked so handsome that her heart almost stopped as she floated to his side.

Love shone out of her eyes, and was reflected back from his in that unique way he had of making her feel truly beautiful.

'You may kiss the bride.'

The ceremony had passed in a poetic blur. Now Terise trembled as Ryan took her in his arms for their first public kiss as man and wife.

Behind her, Trudy tugged at Elaine's hand. 'Grandma, is that 'rassment?'

Elaine coughed in surprise. 'Harassment? Of course it isn't, not when you *want* to be kissed.'

'Daddy says our new mummy has a mouth just asking to be kissed,' Lisa chimed in helpfully.

'Then I s'pose they'll be kissing a lot,' Trudy said.

Against his new bride's mouth, Ryan smiled indulgently. His faintly teasing voice reached her ears alone. 'Out of the mouth of very babes...'

MILLS & BOON

Just Married

Celebrate the joy, excitement and adjustment that comes with being 'Just Married' in this wonderful collection of four new short stories.

Written by four popular authors

Sandra Canfield

Muriel Jensen

Elise Title

Rebecca Winters

Just Married is guaranteed to melt your hearts— just married or not!

Available: April 1996   Price: £4.99

MILLS & BOON

Today's Woman

Mills & Boon brings you a new series of seven
fantastic romances by some of your favourite
authors. One for every day of the week in fact
and each featuring a truly wonderful woman
who's story fits the lines of the old rhyme
'Monday's child is...'

Look out for Patricia Knoll's
Desperately Seeking Annie in April '96.

Thursday's child Annie Parker is recovering
from amnesia when she meets a tall dark
handsome stranger who claims to be her
husband. But how can she spend the rest of her
life with a man she can't even remember—
let alone remember marrying?

Temptation

Coming up in
BACHELOR ARMS...

*When Blythe Fielding planned her wedding and asked
her two best friends, Caitlin and Lily, to be bridesmaids,
none of them had a clue a new romance was around the
corner for each of them—even the bride!*

These entertaining, dramatic stories of friendship, mystery and
love by **JoAnn Ross** continue to follow the exploits of the
residents of Bachelor Arms. If you loved the male Bachelor Arms
titles you'll love the next set coming up in Temptation featuring
the female residents of this lively apartment block.

Look out for:

FOR RICHER OR POORER (March 1996)
THREE GROOMS AND A WEDDING (April 1996)

GET 4 BOOKS
AND A MYSTERY GIFT

Return this coupon and we'll send you 4 Mills & Boon Romances and a mystery gift absolutely FREE! We'll even pay the postage and packing for you.

We're making you this offer to introduce you to the benefits of Reader Service: FREE home delivery of brand-new Mills & Boon romances, at least a month before they are available in the shops, FREE gifts and a monthly Newsletter packed with information.

Accepting these FREE books and gift places you under no obligation to buy, you may cancel at any time, even after receiving just your free shipment. Simply complete the coupon below and send it to:

MILLS & BOON READER SERVICE, FREEPOST, CROYDON, SURREY, CR9 3WZ.

No stamp needed

Yes, please send me 4 free Mills & Boon Romances and a mystery gift. I understand that unless you hear from me, I will receive 6 superb new titles every month for just £2.10* each postage and packing free. I am under no obligation to purchase any books and I may cancel or suspend my subscription at any time, but the free books and gifts will be mine to keep in any case. (I am over 18 years of age)

1EP6R

Ms/Mrs/Miss/Mr _____

Address _____

_____

_____ Postcode _____

Offer closes 30th September 1996. We reserve the right to refuse an application. *Prices and terms subject to change without notice. Offer only valid in UK and Ireland and is not available to current subscribers to this series. **Readers in Ireland please write to: P.O. Box 4546, Dublin 24.** Overseas readers please write for details.

You may be mailed with offers from other reputable companies as a result of this application. Please tick box if you would prefer not to receive such offers. ☐

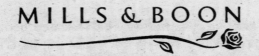

MILLS & BOON

Next Month's Romances

Each month you can choose from a wide variety of romance with Mills & Boon. Below are the new titles to look out for next month.

HOT BLOOD	Charlotte Lamb
PRISONER OF PASSION	Lynne Graham
A WIFE IN WAITING	Jessica Steele
A WOMAN TO REMEMBER	Miranda Lee
SPRING BRIDE	Sandra Marton
DESPERATELY SEEKING ANNIE	Patricia Knoll
THE BACHELOR CHASE	Emma Richmond
TAMING A TYCOON	Leigh Michaels
PASSION WITH INTENT	Natalie Fox
RUTHLESS!	Lee Wilkinson
MY HERO	Debbie Macomber
UNDERCOVER LOVER	Heather Allison
REBEL BRIDE	Sally Carr
SECRET COURTSHIP	Grace Green
PERFECT STRANGERS	Laura Martin
HEART'S REFUGE	Quinn Wilder